I0770932

ARIANA

Pathos, Book 4

2nd Edition

Tamara Henson

Tamara Henson Studios, LLC

Barbourville, KY, USA

Published by Tamara Henson Studios, LLC
Barbourville, KY, USA
www.tamarahenson.com

ISBN-13: 978-1-968677-05-3

DEDICATION

To Diane, whose two cents are worth
a million. She bolstered my spiritual faith when my
heart faltered, shoved me down a path of self-
confidence, and is a great alternate mom!

(Bill...ditto on the above stuff for you, plus you're a
super-special precious alternate dad, too!)

Thanks for being there for me,
and I love you both!

*   *   *

CONTENT NOTICE:

This work mentions and depicts violent parental death
(yes, a running theme!), not addressing severe mental
trauma, some non-explicit romantic heavy petting,
genocide and desecration of a grave. But hey, there's
an awesome bathtub you can swim in, with endless
hot water, and no one wears shoes...ever!

CONTENTS

DEDICATION...V

CONTENT NOTICE: V

1: THE ANGEL...9

2: DREAMER...17

3: MATRIARCH 29

4: THE TRUTH 41

5: WELCOME..73

6: THE JEWELRY BOX 79

7: THE BLOOD RUBY 103

8: BLESSED BLOOD 123

ABOUT THE AUTHOR.....................................143

1: THE ANGEL

Ariana sat on the edge of her bed, gritting her teeth against the familiar ache of her *condition*. The pain washed through her swollen joints and misshapen bones in continual waves that pulsed with each beat of her heart. With a grimace, she lowered her heavy feet to the cold floor and let them settle there. She gathered her strength to stand. With one hand on the edge of the white canopy bed and the other on her cedar nightstand, she pushed her body to an upright position, biting back the whimper that escaped her clenched lips.

Stubbornly, she turned up her nose at the metal walker, snorting at the goofy tennis balls crammed onto the front legs. Passing it up, she threw her weight onto the dresser, then the door frame, then the door, willing her body to do as she said. Twisting the knob quietly and pulling it open on oiled hinges, she glanced down the long hallway toward the restroom. Ariana's long, wavy hair dripped with sweat and plastered around her pallid face. She scowled at the crutches propped right outside her door, and left them in the corner.

She made her way down the hallway, leaning heavily on the wall, and paused occasionally, breathing in gasps with her eyes shut tight. Girls her age didn't cry over minor inconveniences such as this, her parents would tell her. *But most girls my age can walk and laugh and run painlessly*, thought the girl in waves of bitterness. *Girls my age go on dates and worry about makeup and getting their driver's license and their first cars. If only...* Ariana bit down on her lip and stopped the thought. She felt she would sink into a sour darkness if she continued thinking that way. She had not been raised to be bitter and angry. She had been brought up to be strong and quiet, as part of a closeknit nuclear family with no immediate relatives.

Having no other kids in the family, and schooling at home due to her mobility and other medical issues, left her lonesome and awkward. Ariana twisted the doorknob to the bathroom like a lifeline of safety, spilling into the room and closing the door before she turned on the lights.

She sat on the edge of the bathtub, drawing a bath as hot as she could stand. Only the heat soothed her pain for a while, so she bathed often. Even in the middle of the night with the moon high overhead. She pulled her small battery powered radio from a nearby shelf, turning the tiny dial to ON. She fumbled with the volume in a panic, telling it to hush with a hissing voice, and then breathed a sigh of relief when it dropped to a wee-hours level. She liked the crackling imperfection of its distinctive transistor sound, feeling moved by that as much as the smooth oldies she tuned in.

Her parents always worried about her post-midnight "stealth bathing", thinking she'd surely fall asleep and drown. They often forgot she had been a teenager for a while, rendering such possibilities quite unlikely. In a darker mood as the pain slowly eased in her legs, Ariana scoffed. Her pain knew better than to let her go that easily. She snorted, letting the idea of some permanent relief wash over her, no matter how morbid the method. Then she cut that line of thought, pushing it deep for lighter times long after they find a way to heal her body.

Ariana dipped her toes in the steaming water, drawing in a sharp breath at the temperature. Then she plunged one foot in, followed by the other, then slowly, painfully, lowered her body into the bath. The stinging water carried her mind away with the pain, seeking out more normal teenage avenues. Boys, what few she met online or in person, had drawn her interest of late. They often smiled at her face and turned away from her twisting, knobby joints. *Perhaps*, she thought, *it's just as well. I can't go out like this, not truly.* She sighed, as much in relaxation as chagrin.

Struggling out of the water once it cooled had proven the real challenge. Still warm from her bath, and then hot from the exertion of getting up from the bath, Ariana leaned over the sink. She stared sideways at the soapy water swirling down the drain. Tired again, her pain returning, she cupped her hands, splashed the water over her hot face and stared into the mirror. Her pale pink eyes glared back in disgust, reflecting the room's somber earth tones and warm overhead light, a warmth that she did not feel in her heart. *I'm so tired, just sick of it!* She clenched the edge of the sink. *There's no reason for this pain! If it doesn't stop, how can I keep believing in what they taught me?* She squeezed her eyes shut against such reasoning. Her dad's teaching came back to her. *It rains on the just and the unjust.*

Ariana dug her fingers through her wet hair, taking out her frustration in the rough separation of the tangles and knots. Then she brushed her hair smooth, wondering how she could get so tousled in just a few hours of sleep and a careful washing. The strands that slipped between her fingers dried quickly and were fine as silk, each hair translucent more than white, casting a lavender-gray frame around her pixie face and eerie pale eyes.

"Tired faith is a lonely path, they say, but so is this." Ariana set her brush on the sink. Her scalp now sore with her detangling, she sighed, offering a half-hearted prayer. "I don't know how much longer I can believe. So if you're listening, I need something more than tired faith right now."

She turned off her old transistor radio and left the bathroom as quietly as she entered, turning off the light before she opened the door. When she left the bathroom, her scuffling gait woke her parents as she passed their door. She heard someone shuffling toward their door, and cursed for having disturbed them.

"Ariana—dear?" Mother appeared at the door in an instant, making hardly a sound save for the rustling flow of her long nightgown as the folds caught up to her and settled around her ankles. Mother's sweet perfume flowed after her. "Why are you out of bed on your own? And without your crutches? We would have come to help had you called."

Ariana felt guilty, but somehow defiant. She drew a breath to retort on her near-adult age. Then Mother's look of combined worry, pity and concern cut off the words before they came. Mother's afflicted only-child had come to recognize it as anxiety-laden love. Mother's expression so altered the placid, lineless pale face that she seemed a mere specter of the smiling, joyful-eyed woman Ariana remembered dancing with, hand in hand, before the symptoms appeared.

"Jacob, help her!"

Father dug his knuckles into his sleepy eyes and dug through his thick crop of black hair. Then he leveled Ariana with a quiet, concerned scowl. Her lip quivered. After a second, he broke his sad expression and smiled genuinely, still bleary eyed from sleepiness or tearfulness. He reached down a large, calloused hand and ruffled Ariana's hair. Then he lifted her chin with two thick fingers and, grinning into Ariana's pink eyes, said, "It's all right, Love. Annie here's just wantin' to explore her own limits. She'll move mountains one day." He kissed Ariana's forehead. "No harm done."

Ariana's knees gave out at the most inopportune times. This time, she wanted to show them how she'd move mountains one day by bravely continuing on down the hallway without leaning on the wall. Father scooped her up before she hit the floor, well before Ariana's mother had time to cry out. His smooth, steady stride whisked her away down the hallway with her hands clamped together behind his neck and her cheek laid against his tan throat. He whispered loving words in an odd accent that hovered somewhere between Australian and Scottish, having had one of each nationality as his parents. Ariana sighed, content in Father's comforting embrace.

Her mother led the way and swung the door open wide before tidying Ariana's small bed. Mother. Celeste. Love, Father called this beautiful woman. And Angel, too. *Yes*, Ariana thought as she drifted toward sleep, *she looks like an angel—tall and pale and perfect*. The young girl's eyes drifted closed as Father placed her carefully on the straightened sheets, like a china doll that would shatter if jostled. *But why? I'm fourteen years old. I'm practically grown!* The last thing she remembered before she fell into a deep sleep was her mother's cool hand on her forehead. How comforting that touch was to Ariana! The touch drained away all her pain, if only for a while, and she could rest, knowing her mother the angel sat with her.

*   *   *

Back in their bedroom, Celeste sat with her face buried in her hands. She bit her lip and lifted the lid off a carved marble jewelry box. She cupped the end of a long necklace in her hand, clutching it to her breast. Her shoulders shook as she muffled the sobs that wracked her slight frame against Jacob's shoulder. He draped his arm around her shoulders. His face heavier than before, his gray eyes held a burden only his wife understood.

"Were we wrong to take her, Jacob? Can we protect her as she is now?" Celeste heaved a breath, shaking all over.

"She would be dead by now if we stayed. They would've snuffed out her life years ago, and *then* we would have failed!" Jacob squeezed her shoulders. "She has had the chance to live—*away* from your people!"

"But what a life, my husband! My people would have helped us understand! They could have cured her!" Celeste cried, leaning into Jacob's arms.

"Are you so sure this is sickness, my Angel? Hasn't even one of your kind suffered this way?" Jacob pulled her away from his neck and looked into her eyes.

She shook her head. "I learned so little about her before we left, and understood even less of my training there!"

Celeste stared at the small white spear on the end of the necklace. "If only you would speak for me." She gave the tiny spear one last squeeze and replaced it in her jewelry box.

"I have ordered the supplies for the last piece. I should be able to start tomorrow." She cast a wistful glance at Jacob. "A ring, a guide for her path. I see a bird wreathed in flames. She calls out to me, but I can't hear her name. This power, it haunts me even far away from that mountain!"

"Then it's time we tell her. She must understand why she suffers. If her position is so high, we should teach her now." Jacob's kind eyes pleaded with her.

"No!" Her hands dropped from her tear-soaked face in a panic. "I can't put her through that! Tell her what she is and that she'll never know peace? I want to keep my little girl safe! I want her to live free of the destiny they'll force upon her! As long as we can!" Celeste broke down into sobs once more.

"Then we will wait. We will hold her as long as we can, but soon she'll take flight on us, Love. With a spirit like hers, she will soar!"

2: DREAMER

Ariana awoke to mournful cries of the last birds singing farewell to summer. She clung to her dream of fanciful worlds, where pain was abolished and fantastic creatures of all sorts visited Ariana. She frolicked among the wildflowers and twisting trees with them. Her light and graceful steps, like her mother's, carried her barefoot through grass and leaves and moss. She could jump and laugh and sing.

Creatures of myth and legend drifted in her periphery. When she turned to look directly, they would vanish. Only a stately griffin allowed her to look upon him. His somber expression tugged at her heart more than the others. With his talons, he ruffled the head feathers of a vivid orange and golden chick—barely out of the egg—who wobbled boldly toward Ariana. Then leaves rustled in the trees ahead, startling the chick beneath the safety of the griffin's wing.

Ariana stared in shock as another creature emerged from the shadows. Her mouth still ajar, she reached her hand out to the beautiful unicorn that pranced out of the forest, its watery blue eyes imploring. The creature bowed majestically before her. Ariana felt such an empty longing that tore at her chest and left her breathless.

The longing woke her up. Tears streamed down her face as she left those joyful places, suddenly unable to run or jump or even walk without pain. She felt such a loss at having woken up to this imperfect world of hurt. Ariana rubbed the tears from her eyes until her face burned. She decided to stay in bed, so she could dream it all again. Pulling the lavender comforter up over her head to block the sunshine, she turned her head to one side. Another tear slipped down her cheek. Just one more. That's all she would allow.

More dreams came that day, far from the wondrous fantasies she enjoyed during the night. A snake envenomed a woodland water hole. Ariana had to go clean it out. When she finished, the serpent just poisoned it again. Frustrated, she stomped off to find the snake and make it stop, but a loud, sweet voice called to her. A tall lady, with long white hair and a cape waited for her in the forest. When Ariana went to her, she changed into a huge, fanged monster that tried to eat her. As the teeth closed around her painful joints and she was sure to die, she awakened with a start and a scream on her lips. Sweat streaked her face, matted her white hair and dripped into her eyes.

Her bones felt afire, much more excruciating than the constant ache. Her nerves sent shockwaves head to toe like she'd never experienced before. Her skeleton pulsed outward and collapsed inward. She couldn't move. Her swollen joints wouldn't flex. When she tried to move, pain jolted throughout her body. Her heart pounded in her chest. She heard it in her ears. With every beat it shuddered a little, a vibrating tremor that scared her. Ariana screamed and screamed, feeling every moment that she was dying.

Her heartbeat became weaker. Then it shuddered finally to a stop. Ariana felt the churning in her chest as her blood slowed and pooled. The shock robbed her of the breath to scream. Her mind grew fuzzy. The pain dulled, an odd blessing as her mind drifted within her body. Blurry forms of her parents burst into the room, but she couldn't hear them. She couldn't call to them. She slipped quietly into the blackness that welled around her, feeling Death take her into his painless void.

*   *   *

Ariana's eyes opened slowly and focused on white ceiling tiles. Blessed sight! She could smell, too. All around her lingered a distinctive chemical scent. For a while, her body felt numb, and then her skin tingled all over, like when her foot fell asleep while hanging her leg off the bed. Then her entire body awakened. Pinpricks of pain washed over her skin. She ignored the tingling all over. It soon subsided. She remembered vaguely a pain far greater that happened only recently. But something made her memory fuzzy and impeded her thoughts. Her head swam with medicine.

"Mother..." her rough voice rasped. Her sore throat felt like she'd swallowed razorblades. Her dry, cracked lips parted for breath. She wanted water. But she wanted Mother more. Where was she? And Father, too?

A door opened to her right, but her neck wouldn't turn to see it. A short sturdy woman with black hair pulled back in a tight bun and a dark, lined face appeared in her peripheral vision.

"Thank Him, you're awake. And after these many months!" she exclaimed with a thick French accent, waving her hands skyward. "Your parents will be absolutely delighted!"

"Water?" Ariana coughed out. The effort of speaking threatened to drain away any energy she had.

"Of course, child." She pressed an intercom button over Ariana's head.

Ariana heard the flow of water from a pitcher into a cup. Then the lady spoke quickly into the intercom in French. The nurse-lady came to her with a glass and a straw. Then she leaned over Ariana's bed. They had propped her head up and forward, so she opened her lips. She choked on her first two attempts to drink, much to the concern of her nurse. Finally, water flowed down her throat. It felt like she hadn't drunk in ages. She thanked the nurse and asked again for her mother.

"We have called them, child. They should be here soon." The nurse assured her with a pat on her swollen wrist. "We'd only just convinced your mother to go get a bite for the first time this week. It's only the second time she left your side."

Ariana frowned. *These many months*, the nurse had said. *How long exactly?* And her mother had only left twice! Worry filled her mind at the thought of her mother's suffering. So many other emotions welled up that she couldn't sort them out due to the medicine.

"I am Nessa, your nurse." Nessa gave a curt nod. "I've kept watch over you the entire time. Are you comfortable? Is there more I can do? The doctor will be here in a moment to check on your condition. By then, your parents will be near..." She prattled on in a conversational tone as she tidied the small bed and straightened the many machines surrounding her bed.

Still unable to move her head much, Ariana saw several plastic tubes rising from her swollen bare arms. The intravenous units above her dripped all manner of fluids into their insertion points. She could feel very little of them. Her only pain had been the tingle of her body waking up with her mind. Soon, her head began to clear. She recognized the trim around the ceiling, some prints on the wall.

"Hello, Ariana!" The doctor's warm smile lit up her room. "My favorite gift in months is you waking up at long last!"

"Doctor Singleton!" Ariana croaked, glad to recognize her family's physician, who had tried to treat her for so long after other professionals had given up. "What's the damage?"

"Let's see. What pain do you feel?" He pulled out his little notebook and scowled, all business.

"None, really." Ariana shifted her weight. "Just felt fuzzy for a while."

After her initial greeting, Ariana studied the doctor's face as he looked her over and made quick notes and thoughtful scowls. He was old and balding, his face aged but his movements quick and dexterous. She knew him. She watched him, answered when he asked her questions, and tried not to wince when he moved her joints. By the time he was finished with her, he had taken out a few IVs, instructed her to begin eating lightly, and exclaimed at her healthy heart and robust body considering the coma, stressed heart, and 'her condition.'

He patted her head, like he'd done for years. Inwardly, she didn't mind this time. The familiarity touched her. She smiled at him as he turned and left the room. His manipulation of her legs and arms took a toll. The pain medication from a removed IV wore off. The dull ache returned.

A heart attack and a coma, on top of everything else? Ariana sighed. She stared at the ceiling, past the tiles and to where she imagined a blue, clear sky loomed. *You're not helping your case any!*

Moments later, Mother ran into the room and draped across Ariana's swollen body. She forgot her bitterness and crisis of faith in that one joyous moment. When Ariana finally got a look at her mother, she pressed her lips together to keep from crying. Her mother's pale face looked drawn, gaunt with worry. She had lost weight—a danger for someone already thin. Lines fought to etch their way across her smooth forehead.

Ariana hugged her with all her small strength. Her lip quivered. Tears spilled down her cheeks into Mother's pale hair as she reassured the woman that she would be okay. Mother pulled away and looked at her lovingly with eyes another level deeper in worry and sorrow.

"We're sure glad to see you awake, Annie. You gave us one 'ell of a scare." Father kissed her cheek and ruffled her hair.

His smile beamed down with the warmth of the sun, his kind eyes on his little girl. She basked in the love from both parents and vowed to herself to get better. She would recover from this, then face her aggressive bone overgrowth—or whatever it was—so that nothing about 'her condition' would worry her parents anymore. She vowed to be cured, so nothing could take her from her parents again. After all, she'd fought Death, and beat him this once, so she had nothing to fear. Her resolve was set on being able to run, to walk, to dance hand in hand with her mother once again in the meadow. Nothing could stop her now!

A few days in the small hospital and more painful physical therapy granted Ariana permission to return home. Dr. Singleton had insisted on one more night to monitor a minor heart murmur that had him concerned for years. This last night, Ariana felt joyous, though aching from the hours spent with nurses rotating and bending her joints. Her parents even staked out sleeping cots in her room to leave quite early the next morning for the long trip back home. All the IVs had been removed with the holes bandaged and healing. The only remaining machinery attached to her was the cardiac monitor. The cold electrodes warmed against her chest. In her happiness she could ignore them.

Mother sat beside her on the mattress and stroked her hair. Father sat bedside in a leather recliner, leaning forward with his elbows on his knees and smiling in a relieved, sleepy way. Mother tucked the sheets and blanket around Ariana and glanced at her husband, who took her hand lovingly.

"I have feared for your safety all your life, with many good reasons." Her mother-angel stroked Ariana's hair. "Now, I realize the strength of our ancient blood rushes through your veins. I realize you will be strong enough to conquer this condition. I realize just how much power you have inside to live no matter what. I finally begin to accept your *destiny*, dearest Ariana, when I ran so long from it." She whispered into her sleepy daughter's ear, with her husband pursing his lips in deep thought nearby.

"But I don't know if I believe," Ariana murmured. But the words sounded garbled. "I don't know."

"Hmmm? Of course you don't know, dear. Tomorrow," Celeste said, "we will teach you everything you need to know."

"We can only protect you from fate so long, Annie. Whatever happens in your future, know that we love you always, and can never be gone from you. We'll be here," and her father tapped above an electrode, "and we'll keep that heart beating ourselves if we have to."

Ariana drifted off to sleep before they finished. Their words felt like a dream that swelled her heart with a battling combination of joy and confusion. She mumbled, "I love you, too" as she fell into the velvety press of peaceful sleep where pain rarely followed.

The vibrantly colorful world of beautiful legendary creatures swirled around her. Then she felt a tugging at her foot. Something heavy and cold slipped over it, moving up her leg and behind it. Ariana felt fear. The heaviness twined around her legs, up and around her hips. She opened her eyes in the darkness and looked down. Shiny green-black coils wrapped higher and higher around her body, pushing her torso up to curve beneath her then lying over her body. She was paralyzed with fear. *Or is this another dream?*

When at last the snake-body immobilized her shoulders, she yelled for her parents. At that moment, the snake's body began to constrict, cutting off her breathing. Her body began to collapse in on itself in waves of pain. Her mouth screamed soundlessly when the huge head of the snake wound from behind her and settled its cold, evil gaze on her face. A long tongue flicked in and out, and long fangs needled out from the broad head. It began to open its mouth.

*　　　*　　　*

The nurse, Nessa, looked up from her paperwork when an erratic beeping sounded from the computer. Her heavy dark eyes widened. Ariana's heart monitor was reading off the charts! With prior heart problems, she would die if they didn't act fast. The nurse ran into the doctor's office and shook him awake where he dozed with his head on his desk. Both set out at a run for Ariana's room, the nurse explaining on the way. Both hoped they were not too late.

*　　　*　　　*

Celeste and Jacob awoke at the erratic beeping of their daughter's heart monitor, wondering what horrible thing had happened in such a short time for her heart to be so irregular and fast. They rushed to her bedside, holding out their hands, ready to do... something! She was immobile. Sweat poured down her face and soaked her gown. Her father pressed the nurse's button several times.

Ariana seemed at one time to whisper their names, at another to mumble, then she was quiet, but her mouth moved in horror. Her parents grabbed her, shook her, and tried to wake her to no avail. Her body was rigid, as if held in position by some other power.

"He's already here. He's found her! Show yourself, you coward!" Celeste stared all around. She felt an intangible power spill outward with her words.

For an instant, gray shadows in the room manifested and Celeste could see it clearly. A great serpent coiled around her daughter. It locked its cold eyes on Celeste in defiance. How had it crept onto this plane, far from the source of its power? How could it maintain ethereal form without its true master? Unless, Celeste reasoned, this is the monster incarnate, claiming her life himself!

"Be gone, beast! She is my daughter! My life!" She clawed at the serpent. Her hands touched only air. The creature then returned its gaze to Ariana's agonized face.

From there, the visible form dissipated. It still lingered there, squeezing the life out of Ariana. Jacob clung to his daughter with trembling hands. He could not grasp the creature. He hadn't even seen it as his wife had. He froze during his futile struggle. In the dim light, Ariana's skin became luminous with more than sweat. At each swollen joint, light gathered and pulsed. Her face became illuminated by an unnatural glow.

"And here I stand, weak!" Celeste stared at the light, disgusted by her own frailty. She dug in her heels and forced herself not to take a step back. "Jacob, it's too late. You're right! It's not a sickness. It's a defense!" Celeste wrung her hands, helpless. "Fleeing didn't help in the end, just delayed him. He will kill her if he can. But even if she survives, her heart cannot! She will die!"

The woman who was called Angel and Love gazed with fear into her husband's eyes. Jacob pressed his lips firmly together. Then he nodded his dark head. His arms wrapped around his wife as together they looked upon their weakened daughter with clear knowledge of her *condition*. He kissed his wife deeply and desperately, then spoke with deep resolve.

"Then we'll have to fix her heart, like we promised." His eyes were stern with concentration. "I may be only human, Love, but I have a father's determination."

Celeste gazed into his eyes, then spread her hands across her daughter's ribcage. "Please be enough." She wavered on her feet, gathering her remaining strength.

"It will be, my Love." Jacob placed his large, calloused hands over his Angel's hands. The woman closed her eyes and bent over in concentration. Weak light emanated from the mother-angel's hands. The glow spread and sank into Ariana's chest. The light faded in her mother's pallid features as her husband watched. Jacob then lifted up his own voice, his only power.

"Our dear Heavenly Father, praise be to you for the lives you give us. God please help them, for I know each of us has a purpose in your eyes and in your plan. I rebuke this evil that takes my daughter's peace, and pray..."

The fervent prayer went on as light faded from his sweet wife and light poured from his daughter. Tears flowed down his cheeks as he spoke to his Master. His wife, his Love, lifted her head feebly. A smile of deepest love lit her now colorless lips. For her husband, and for her daughter.

"We have given her life, by His power, once again, my husband." Celeste shuddered, feeling the chill creep into her flesh. "The cost, though, may be very great. But we will be with her," the mother whispered.

Jacob faltered in his words to listen to the woman he loved. Then she collapsed into his arms, having given all she had so that their daughter would live. His tears flowed. Sobs wracked his body. Through his pain he spoke out once more.

"Father, watch over our dear daughter. Keep her safe and ease her heart. Father, forgive us our sins and let us always stay together. I want to go with her, Lord. Please. In His name, Amen..." he broke down into sobs as light from his daughter flooded the room.

He clung to his unconscious wife with one arm and laid one hand on his child. The next seconds were an eternity. Jacob's legs wouldn't move. He needed to get away. He saw nothing around his ankles, but felt the cold, tight pressure constrict, holding him in place.

Frozen in place, he held his wife by his side and trembled with fury. *You're taking her father away from her, too?* He clenched his fists. *She will be far stronger than you one day, monster, and she will come for you!*

Jacob stared in awe as white spirals burst through Annie's knees and elbows and shoulders and everywhere her joints had kept her immobile. They twined slowly outward, formed a point, and dug into cloth and metal with equal ease. Jacob watched the milky white spiral split the smooth forehead of his daughter. It stopped and the glow shone brightly on trickling blood from the spines of twining overgrowth. He smiled with love and laid a rough hand aside his daughter's face. He stroked her cheek tenderly. He leaned awkwardly over her and kissed her cheek.

"We love you, girl. We're with you. Don't forget it, my little Annie!"

*   *   *

Then everything blurred with startling light that filtered under the door into the hallway. Nessa and Dr. Singleton skidded to a stop, confused. Heavy, sharp thuds rattled the door on its hinges. Glass shattered. The doctor's hand hesitated on the doorknob. Then they burst through into the room. Nessa stared in shock and crossed herself. She babbled a prayer and forced herself to stop hyperventilating. Spikes of a spiral white substance stabbed into the walls, through curtains and mirrors all over the room.

Crumpled in each other's arms at bedside laid Jacob and Celeste. Dr. Singleton rushed over, checking for pulses and pressing his lips together when he found none. The same spikes drilled into their bodies. He couldn't deny that the white spears had ultimately caused their deaths. *But why didn't they move?*

Seeing the bodies, Nessa began screaming in horror. The doctor grabbed her and shook her. "We were warned! These wonderful people warned us! We have our instructions from them in case such a thing happens." He released her shoulders.

"But she did this? She killed them!" Nessa shrieked. "Her own parents!"

"That's enough! Not another word!" Dr. Singleton punctuated his point by slamming his fist against the nearby table. "We were told who and what she was when she came here. And we were told in confidence! So get your supplies together and help treat her or she'll bleed to death!" He pointed with an old, gnarled finger to the shivering figure clothed in a hole-pocked gown and much of her red blood.

Nessa clenched her jaw and walked to where the girl lay. Ariana's dismayed eyes froze on her dead parents, over whom the doctor leaned, checking again with fleeing hope for vitals. A wordless horror darkened her stricken face. She made no sound when the nurse treated and bandaged her open wounds. The nurse was unable to provide a suitable comfort, and even less inclined to do so given the situation, so she worked in silence.

Nessa concentrated on the major wounds, each at the juncture of a joint. Each wound formed a quarter-moon shape with slits leading outward from the center that looked like a starburst pattern. The little wounds on her hands and smaller joints formed tiny stars. As she worked, the smaller wounds already seemed to be sealing themselves up, as if spontaneous healing took place. The swelling had gone. The cause of the swelling seemed very obviously embedded around the room. Nessa's hands trembled in fear.

3: MATRIARCH

Ariana remained in the hospital. They moved her to a new room. The fresh room had bright Van Gogh sunflower prints and clean off-white walls. New nurses attended to her. She hadn't seen Nessa since that horrible night.

"But she did this? She killed them!" Nessa had screamed. *"Her own parents!"*

The scene never left her mind. She still saw the old hospital room with her parents crumpled by her bedside, cradled in each other's arms. Stabbed through by something that erupted from their daughter. *I did this.* Ariana stared at their fresh blood on the floor, even though it was long gone in another room. *I killed them.*

She had not spoken a word since her parents' deaths at her hands. She felt numb with guilt and overwhelmed with sadness at the loss. She stayed awake as long as she could, fearing her dreams. Nightmares had been few, to her surprise. But then she would be swept away into bright places where she didn't want to be. After all her suffering and dreaming, her parents couldn't join her there. The following days blended into numbness and heartache.

Her chronic aches and pains vanished. She awoke each morning and took several minutes to realize why she felt physically different. The throbbing agony felt so familiar to her that when it ceased, she almost missed it. In fact, she wished she could feel the pain again. She stared at the knife next to her uneaten meals with a crazy eye so often that the nurses no longer provided her one. Her meats all came neatly sliced beforehand. What atonement could she have on earth for her sin? When once she longed to run and dance, she now felt guilty for her new freedom of movement. She kept still by choice. She couldn't allow herself yet.

Ariana often inspected her now-thin white wrists and narrow legs. She dropped her eyes to her hands. The joints were so fine and delicate-looking, like her mother's. Tears burst from her eyes when she thought about Mother and Father. Then she bit them back. Over the past few days, she remembered more and more of what they had said to her. Their sacrifice helped sober her a little. She wished to know more. But she knew of no one who could help. Didn't deserve their help.

Her fingers brushed her forehead scar as she wiped her tears. She jerked her hands away. Already healed, the pink scars covering her body still disturbed Ariana. She felt her forehead again, deliberately tracing the edges. The scar appeared in the middle of her brow. The same shape as the others, it had sent pink tendrils of the starburst pattern across her left eyebrow, very near her eye. Perhaps it would blind her, if that one appeared again. She shivered and willed that never to happen again, remembering the long spirals and the blood. All the spikes had apparently been taken for some use or research. Her doctor had yet to give the occurrence a title. She only had fanciful speculation as to the meaning of it all.

The door to her room opened, breaching her self-imposed prison. Dr. Singleton stuck his head in to check on her. Seeing her awake, he entered.

"I'm glad to see you up, child. And moving a bit, too, eh?" He smiled an old smile, feeling helpless to heal her mental injuries and painfully aware he'd been capable of little involving her physical maladies as well. He hesitated to give her his current news.

She stared at him in morose silence.

"Your departed parents, rest their souls, left

information that I was to use in such a case as this. You, dear Ariana, are far more special than you know. They fled all they ever knew when your mother gave birth to you, thinking they could protect you from what they had learned." He sat on the edge of the leather armchair next to her bed. Then he paused, drawing a deep breath. "But you have more family, those whom I was to contact when the time came. Custody lies with them. The law has provided for your parents' wishes."

He rose from where he had seated himself and strode to the door. He beckoned to someone in the hallway. The beautiful woman who entered had long white hair pulled back into a loose braid. She looked very young, only slightly older than Mother. Her pale skin and blue eyes bore such a likeness to Celeste that Ariana burst into tears. Her hand froze where it had been tracing the forehead scar. Her jaw dropped open. That there was a family relation could not be denied. But Ariana sat in stunned silence.

"This is your aunt. Your mother's sister. Her name is Gwendolyn Alcourne, from the northern high country. She will watch over you now." The good doctor paused at the door. "I'll give you a few minutes."

With that he took his leave. The thin woman stood quietly, a slight smile lighting her lips. The sadness in her eyes betrayed that smile. She moved with the grace of Ariana's mother and sat on the bedside chair. Then her voice flowed with the grace of her body.

"Aren't you a vision of beauty after these many years, my dear Ariana!" Gwendolyn reached out to Ariana for an official greeting. Ariana reluctantly took the woman's hand. Her silken touch lulled Ariana into a haze of comfort, soothing her with the memory of her mother's hand.

"We each grieve the loss of your mother and father. Celeste was one of our dearest family members. So few of our blood remain." Gwendolyn sat in the bedside armchair. "Fear not for their final rest, for we have arranged for their burial in our homeland, in the place you will arrive soon." Gwendolyn sighed deeply, placing Ariana's hand back on the blanket. "So much of your mother is in your eyes. And I'd thought they would deepen in color, like your mother's did. But a lovely shade of pink they have remained!" Ariana blushed. Gwendolyn's voice had a lilting quality she liked, a high-country dialect and a touch of something else, something older. "Her love flows through your very body. So does that of your father."

Ariana dropped her head. She allowed the woman to wipe her tears away with a lace-edged handkerchief.

Gwendolyn paused, clearly hurting and unsure of whether she should continue. "You want to understand what happened. It plagues your mind. So I will tell you, and I ask you to keep an open mind," she began, her decision made.

Ariana nodded, though her mind roiled with confusion.

"Our people develop a coating over their bones." Gwendolyn gauged Ariana's initial reaction before continuing. The girl merely nodded, all business. "Your coating became an overgrowth because it developed more rapidly than anyone else's ever had. When it got to a certain point, the body reached its limit, and some mental event triggered the uncontrollable release of the overgrowth."

She cringed. Having her parents' deaths reduced to some scientific procedural sickened her. Ariana gulped. In the end, she preferred the direct manner of Gwendolyn to the ignorance of the doctors. But some sort of overgrowth? And what did she mean by *our people. We're all just people, right?*

"What triggered it, Ariana?" Gwendolyn had a softness in her voice. "If you're ready to tell me, I'm ready to listen."

Ariana lowered her head, breathing deeply. She forced down the image of her dead parents long enough to answer. Then she broke her long silence.

"I dreamed of a huge snake squeezing the life out of me. I wanted it to go away, to leave us alone. But it was still there when I opened my eyes, staring at me. My mother and father couldn't see it. I didn't want it to hurt them, so I pushed it. I willed it to die." Ariana curled her knees to her chest and hugged them. "But then my heart felt weird and I forgot what I was doing. But my parents were there. Mother put blue light into my chest and they talked to me. Then I blacked out. When I woke up, the snake was gone. Then I saw my parents on the floor." She trembled. "I think I hurt the snake. I could see dark blood on me that wasn't mine. The nurses couldn't see it, but it was there. I couldn't wash it off."

"You haven't told anyone else, have you?"

Ariana shook her head. "I didn't want them to put me away for being crazy."

"I assure you, dear child," Gwendolyn said, stroking Ariana's hair, "you are not crazy and this is not the last time you'll encounter such darkness."

"There's a chance that it could happen again?" Ariana asked in a too-loud voice, the fear foremost in her mind.

"No." Gwendolyn leveled her eyes on Ariana. "The overgrowth is a one-time-only side effect. You would have to use your will to manifest it again. And you'll learn so much more about that back home."

"A side effect? Of what?"

"Of your parent's decision to take you away, to protect you far away from home." Gwendolyn sighed. "I know what you're thinking, and you didn't kill them. Your parents made a choice. They fully knew the consequences and possibilities that could arise. And that blue light you saw? Your mother and father healed your heart so that you could live to fulfill your purpose."

Ariana caught her breath and fought off sobs. "How do you know about my purpose? Who are you?"

"Family," Gwendolyn replied in a tone that puzzled Ariana to the point of silence. "One of many. Tell me about the spikes?"

Ariana stared out the window. *Many? I have family?* She forced back the faces of her mother and father. "The spears?" Ariana said, her voice trailing off. "They looked like a unicorn's horn."

Gwendolyn paused with a knowing smile. "Indeed they did, dear one. We will discuss everything in depth after your journey, when you are safe at your new home. Perhaps you can tell me about any dreams that have disturbed you lately, as well."

This Gwendolyn Alcourne emanated knowledge and peace. Ariana couldn't help but feel encouraged alongside her grief. Her little town held no reason for staying, with her parents dead, and soon to be buried in a faraway place—the place where Ariana would live. Gwendolyn brought her from the hospital, after she thanked the doctor and nurses who treated her. Ariana gave her best to the absent Nessa as well. Then Gwendolyn drove Ariana to her old cottage.

Ariana fell into silence again. If her parents gave her a new start, she needed to try. Happiness felt far away from her, but perhaps contentment could be achieved. Ariana packed her clothes, some slightly ill-fitting since they didn't have to slip over aching joints anymore. She packed necessities and old toys and her mother's jewelry box and trinkets with a bittersweet remembrance of life in those rooms. Her aunt handled all the details. Everything else in the house had been packed. Someone hammered a "For Sale" sign into the landscaped front yard. This little haven in England no longer felt like her home. The life had left it.

Ariana walked for the last time down the hallway, past her parents' old room and the bathroom. She paused, holding the box with her mother's belongings in it and a backpack on her shoulder. An odd feeling stopped her, a feeling of mobility. For the first time in years she walked the hallway without leaning on furniture and grimacing in pain. Her eyes blurred with tears. A warm current of air flowed around her body. Her heart pounded. And vividly, she saw her mother and father standing over her bed: odd blue light flowed from her mother into Ariana's chest while her father prayed. They smiled with love and embraced until the very end.

"Thank you," Ariana whispered. "Thank you so much."

Sadness briefly lifted, and heart filled with more than life, Ariana stepped out of the hallway, ready to leave the house forever. She wasn't leaving behind anything she needed. All she needed rested inside her.

Gwendolyn smiled and ducked out the front door with her last load in hand for the rental vehicle. The child would be fine now. Ariana could move on in time, with her parents' love to guide her.

*   *   *

Mostly flat land and symmetrically planted forests eventually gave way to rolling hills and naturally grown woodland. Ariana fell asleep several times, unsure whether she had imagined a couple changes of cars and a couple ferry rides during the long trip. The roads curved into evening mist illuminated by the setting sun. Trees crowded the roadway the farther she rode. Finally, the vehicle turned up a cobbled driveway barely wide enough for two cars. Cherry trees draped in pink blooms, mimosa fronds with tufts of pink and white flowers, and weeping willows sprouting new leaves bent their branches overhead, creating a fragrant tunnel of thick foliage through which streamed silver beams of moonlight.

"A bit early for the trees to bloom and sprout, I would think." Ariana's eyes drank in the moonlit beauty, wondering at the silvered edges of soft pink and spring green.

"All flowers seem to bloom early and stay long in this area." Gwendolyn's blue eyes glinted in the dim light. Ariana caught the woman's wry smile in a sideways glance.

Ariana curled up in the front seat, silent from then on out, as her aunt wound the vehicle up a mountain with foliage blocking her view of much else. And still she stared, sleepy eyes forced wide, waiting for this new experience to take flight somehow. All these odd and intriguing sights, all the new events unfolding! All more than she hoped for, and far more than she deserved.

She couldn't imagine that life here would be as amazing as her healed heart and the love of her parents. After all, she had one of the best gifts in the world—life, given by her mother twice in her life, and manifested so purely in her father's love. With trembling resolve, she accepted their final gift of love. Her eyes clouded over as she thought about them. Her head drooped against her arm, propped on the ridge by the window. She fell into a misty, dreamless sleep.

Vaguely, she felt the car roll to a stop some time later. She felt groggy and tired from her ordeal, from forcing herself to stay awake. Her body claimed much needed rest. The fragrant air wafted through the night. A sense of calm and peace washed over her.

Bleary eyes opened on a large, illuminated house, many storied and warmly lit with flickering light from within. The structure took hardly a sharp angle or rough outline, and appeared carved into the living rock of the mountain. Vines of pale wisteria clung to its walls and trailed around large windows. A surreal air of deep nostalgia crept into Ariana's sleepy mind. The garden lay smothered in weeping vines and trees. Pale flowers glowed in the moon's brightness. Everything seemed too expansive to fit on a mountain. Yet it fit, looking far too natural to be manmade. Like art.

"Reminds me of a fairy-tale, or my dreams," muttered Ariana. "I've arrived in a storybook world!"

"It won't always be a fairy-tale for you, dear child. But now, for as long as you are allowed, you may live the life in your dreams." Gwendolyn kissed Ariana's cheek, leaving a pale blue glow where her lips touched. "And now, you must sleep. Rest peacefully, for you are safe. You are in the home where you belong, for now, until you claim your home of purpose far away."

Ariana slept, feeling relaxed and dazed. She drifted off just as several men and women poured out of the house with candelabra. They swiftly unpacked the vehicle. She caught a glimmer of their pale hair and pale skin and light eyes. Just like her mother's. Just like hers.

*   *   *

A tall youth with vibrant emerald-green eyes and wavy silver hair gathered her in his arms and carried her through the double doors of the Mansion-in-the-Mountain. He whisked her up marble stairs and down intricate ivory-laced corridors to a bedroom. The door swept open. A candle glowed inside. The tulle-draped canopy bed stood in the center of the large space with walls covered in dreamy woodland murals. The covers were turned down. Smiling, the young man settled Ariana's sleeping form on the bed and pulled the downy blankets across her body, leaving only her face and shoulders visible. He sighed. The candlelight flickered in his green eyes. He brushed back a lock of silver-gray hair and grinned.

"Sweet dreams, Ariana." He breathed in her soft perfume, then turned to leave. "Perhaps we can get to know each other this time."

Gwendolyn appeared in the doorway as the boy prepared to walk out. "My sister always loved you, Silvan!" She draped an arm across his shoulders. "But you were small when you asked to be newborn Ariana's protector. You may not be able to protect her where she needs to go."

"I was three then. I made it to seventeen knowing that she would return one day, and here she is." Silvan smiled at Gwendolyn. "I still feel the same. I have waited for the chance to protect her, whatever path she follows," Silvan said with pride. He smiled back at Ariana's peaceful, scarred face. "She is perfect, Gwendolyn. I want to keep her safe, no matter what. Then perhaps she won't need to leave."

"Young man, she is not for us to keep, like a statue." Gwendolyn gestured to the garden. "She will go where fate takes her. Even so, she knows not an inkling of her own blood yet."

Silvan smiled a wistful smile and looked into Gwendolyn's blue eyes. "We'll tell her about the ancient race inhabiting this mountain range," here he gestured expansively, "all our secrets and stories. And we'll let her choose for herself."

"Sometimes I forget you're wise beyond your years, brat." Gwendolyn laid a cool hand on his shoulder. "I wonder though. Will it be too much fantasy for a girl raised among stark humanity?"

"She just needs to have some imagination, Aunt Gwen." Silvan curled his lip and shrugged, full of mischief. "Leave the convincing to me!"

Silvan's eyes glinted with mischief and delight. He cast a wide smile at Gwendolyn, then excused himself with a wave. Having Ariana back among her people and the bittersweet sadness of burying Celeste warred inside him. What a deep resolve, and enduring devotion!

The Alcourne blood dwindled over generations. She worried about the level of sacrifice dear Silvan may commit in his duties. Their people were so few in recent decades. And her knowledge of the darkest prophecies heralded a new existence for everyone, or no existence at all, depending on the choices made by the sleeping child before her. Whether good or bad, her decisions served a more basic, greater purpose that even Gwendolyn could not predict. Gwendolyn snuffed out the candle. The gray smoke curled up toward the ceiling. Her eyes followed as it dissipated, and then returned to the exhausted Ariana.

"Onward we plummet into the darkness of our past," she whispered, "to bring forth a pure light."

She left silently, her long dress the only disturbance to the air. Ariana slept on.

4: THE TRUTH

Ariana awoke in cushioned comfort. A dream of soft moonlight on pale faces in a beautiful garden graced her mind and followed her to wakefulness. She awoke to white translucent fabric draped on an unfamiliar canopy bed and a masterful mural painted on stone walls. Light surrounded her from windows above, illuminating the pearlescent dresser top and vanity table. Familiar items rested on the surface, chief among them her mother's jewelry box. Oddly, it seemed to match the room, as if it belonged here. Waking fully, she knew this room had to be in that mansion built into the mountain. Her dream was a reality. And she had missed out on part of it.

Pouting and a little grumpy, she pushed back the downy comforter and glanced around, uncertain of her next step. She stood and turned toward the dresser. On a chair next to the dresser set a wide, flat box with a note atop that read: "A gift, to begin your new life here." Signed by Gwendolyn, in an elegant, dainty script. Ariana pulled off the white top of the box. Inside she found new clothes, made of finely woven soft cloth. A pair of tan breeches hemmed snugly to the knee. A vibrant cornflower blue blouse, with a long hem and flared sleeves, split on top from shoulder to wrist with a tie at the elbow, completed the outfit. Fresh undergarments and a belt to go over the tunic completed her ensemble. She searched for house slippers or shoes, or even socks. Finding none, she headed for the door.

Ariana couldn't guess how long she slept, and wanted the restroom and a bath badly. Still in her travel clothes, she crept to the door and pulled it open a crack, then peeked out. She jumped at the sight of a tall youth lounging on a bench outside her door. He read a heavy book with rapt interest. This he deposited upon seeing her and, grinning, stood up.

"My name is Silvan, Lady Ariana." He executed a formal bow. "I am to help you with anything you need should you wake up, and here you are!"

"I...I... You know me already." Suddenly self-conscious, Ariana wanted very much to cover the scar on her forehead with her hand. She forced her hands in front of her waist. She intently studied the backs of her clenched hands and the window and the wall, throwing her gaze anywhere but into the intense, handsome face of the young man named Silvan.

"Oh, yes." Silvan's tone sounded oddly possessive. "I've known you forever."

She stared up at him then, her eyes wide with apprehension and a little fascination. His smiling eyes sparkled in bright green, his skin almost as pale as hers. His silver-gray hair framed his face and drifted to his shoulders in chunky layers. High cheekbones offset a thin, strong jaw. Below his refined and narrow nose, his gorgeous smile dimpled his cheeks. What a beautiful creature to behold! She felt her face brighten with a blush.

"You probably want to know where the restroom is." He smiled, noticing the redness of her cheeks.

He boldly led her with a gentle hand on her shoulder to the door she needed. "There are 'the facilities' inside on the left, and far to the right are rooms to shower or bathe. Gwendolyn left you all the things you'd need, including a blue robe when you're finished."

"Are you, um, gonna…wait?" Ariana's cheeks felt on fire.

"If need be." He teased with a grin. "If not, I'll be back in an hour to get you. By then, you'll be hungry, too."

He jogged off down the hallway, with his silver hair bobbing and his right hand grasping the thick book she caught him reading, a finger holding his place about halfway through. When he turned a corner, Ariana lifted her jaw and closed her gaping mouth, realizing she had been staring at this strange young man who acted like he'd known her all her life. *Was he family?* Secretly, she hoped not.

She pulled the door open and went inside. The toilet area appeared standard enough, with only a few flowing carvings in the wash basins and stalls. When she had made use of certain facilities, she sought out the bathing area. The short hallway led to an ivory and violet gray cove of etched stone partitions. Each stone arch opened on a separate bathing area. Elegant sculptures of tree trunks, stones and vines made every surface more organic. Ariana let her hands wander over the smooth texture of leaves and the rough bark. She marveled at the shapes that had been cut from the mountain stone. Light filtered in from skylights a fair distance above her, playing over the marbled violet and white around her.

She located the spacious cubicle with a smallish blue robe hanging beside and pulled the cloth curtain across behind her. The huge tub basin sank into the floor with steps leading down past the seating ledge to the smooth base. She fiddled with the ornate knobs at shoulder level on the wall until the deep tub began to fill with steaming water. Bath soaps and oils ranged on a raised shelf at the back of the pool. She discarded her sleep-grimy clothes on the floor. She decided it would be a waste to fill the tub all the way for someone as slight as her, so she cut off the water. Ariana dipped a pale toe in water hot enough to pink her skin, and briefly remembered her late-night baths to ease her pain.

Finding the water familiar and to her liking, she stepped into the thigh-deep bath and reached for the unfamiliar bath oils and soaps. New and intoxicating aromas made it difficult to choose from the provided selections. When she found one she preferred, the scent tugged at her memory until she shuddered, clenching the unlabeled bottle of liquid soap. *Mother, where do you get your perfume?* Ariana had asked a long time ago. *Oh, here and there,* Mother had replied. *I want to smell just like you do!* Ariana had said. *Maybe when you're all grown up,* she had said with a sad smile. She breathed in the unique scent of Mother's soap and perfume and felt like crying all over again.

"Mother." Ariana blinked back her tears and focused on bathing. All the while her mother's scent flowed around her. She had to use the soap liberally to wash off the feeling of dirt. She scrubbed the oil out of her pale hair until the strands squeaked. She soaped a rough washcloth and scoured all the scars her body had inflicted upon itself until they were much pinker. The slight stinging reminded her again of her years in pain and hot baths and doctors shaking their heads in defeat.

Ariana sank onto the ledge built into the side of the pool. She let the heat soak into her sorrow-chilled bones, closing her eyes with a sigh. When her fingers wrinkled and the water cooled, she had taken one of the most luxurious and much-needed baths ever in her life. Some of the pain of losing her parents, some of the personal guilt she carried, flowed down the drain with her bathwater.

She toweled off, pausing at each half-moon-and-starburst scar that adorned her pale body. She slipped into the soft robe, her heart calmed for the moment. Ariana pushed back the steam-dampened curtain of her bathing cubicle and headed for the door. Only then did the stirrings of hunger begin. Her stomach growled as she entered the hallway and padded barefoot to her new room. Silvan stood in the hallway, facing a window. One shoulder supported his weight, his arms crossed in mock, or real, boredom. He grinned out the window. He didn't glance her way. Protecting my modesty? she mused.

"Gwendolyn said it might take you a while, so I figured an hour would suffice. I have been firmly reminded that women and bubble baths seem to take a bit longer than that." He struggled to keep the smile off his face.

"I...I'm so sorry. I didn't mean to inconvenience you, Silvan." Ariana stared down at her clenched hands again. "I apparently slept longer than I thought, and really needed..."

Then he turned to her and she stopped short. His green eyes glinted. "And you remember my name, too. Somehow it's prettier when spoken by you."

*   *   *

His cheeks blazed at his comment. Then he blushed again when he remembered she wore only a robe. He gasped and caught her eyes with his. The pink in her irises looked darker in the hall lighting. Then he turned away, his face obscured by silver-gray locks of hair.

"Anyway, I told you I was here to help you. Part of that was waiting." He crossed his arms again. "And I intend to hang around just as long as I have to, Ariana, to do my job."

In his peripheral vision, her head bowed in embarrassment. Silvan thought he heard her say "Thanks." Then she slipped into her room. Silvan breathed again, willing his heartbeat to slow. He found it difficult to be so casual around someone he'd cared about for so long.

"Yes," he whispered. "I've waited most of my life. You're here now, so it doesn't feel like waiting anymore."

*   *   *

Safely behind the door of her room ,she slumped against the sturdy, carved wood, fumbling to latch the knob. Her face felt hot despite the cool damp hair that clung to her cheeks. She allowed her heart to slow down and the slight tremors in her limbs to subside. Finally, she brushed her wet hair and pulled it into a loose braid so it could continue to dry, albeit slowly, and found a ribbon to tie around the end. She dressed quickly in the blue shirt and tan pants, then fastened the belt around her waist. Searching all around the white room, Ariana couldn't find a pair of shoes. Resigned, she opened the door.

"Wow, record time!" Silvan turned to look at her, a smile akin to pride and closer to adoration crinkling his emerald eyes and dimpling his cheeks.

Silvan stepped forward and offered his arm, fully a gentleman. She placed her hand in the crook of his elbow with some hesitation. He led her down long hallways and spiraling stairs to a main hall. They spoke little, until Ariana's curiosity won over.

"I couldn't find my shoes. I need them." She kicked up her bare foot and wiggled her toes for emphasis.

"Why?" he teased, smiling down at her. "Nothing on this mountain will harm your tender feet. Even the bugs know how important you are." Then he laughed a little, shy and awkward suddenly.

She wilted under his good humor. Everyone seemed to know everything she didn't, and no one had told her anything. Her pace slowed as she dove into her thoughts. Silvan noticed and looked at her.

"I didn't mean to upset you," he said softly.

"Oh, no. You haven't. It's just my ignorance, I suppose."

"Gwendolyn will tell you everything she knows tonight. But not until you've eaten, young lady!"

With that, he marched her along more briskly, into a high-ceilinged, oblong room. A huge table occupied the center, crafted from a giant cross-section slab of some ancient tree with irregular edges all around and a gleaming oiled surface. Marveling at the innumerable concentric rings, she couldn't count enough of them to estimate the age of such a huge tree, let alone how they could've managed to get it inside the solid stone walls.

Ariana smelled food cooking at that moment, and forgot the impressive table. The aroma passed her nose and reached her empty stomach, which roared in the silence. The cavernous room seemed to echo with the sound. Her face burned with embarrassment.

"I had hoped, Silvan, that you'd bring her to dine before she starved to death!" echoed a voice at the far end of the room.

The dark figure busily lit heavy candles on massive candelabra along the back wall. Then she lit candles along the table. She stoked a hearth fire, which roared, knocking off the midday chill of the sunless room. As they approached, the figure turned. Gwendolyn smiled in the yellow glow of the firelight. She gestured for Ariana to sit. Silvan rushed to pull out the heavy high-backed chair for her at the far corner of the table, then claimed his chair beside her. Gwendolyn sat at the head of the table with such regality it seemed she sat there often.

"The afternoon meal will be served soon, child. I know you have questions, Ariana. We'll answer the big ones later, but for now." Her voice trailed off.

"Will many be eating here tonight?" Ariana stared wide eyed along the circumference of the huge table.

"Not wanting to make a public show of yourself

yet, dear? Quite understandable. No, is the answer. We'll not have the entire household filled until you're ready. Everyone knows that, so they've made themselves scarce. Except for one fellow," she nodded to Silvan, "who insisted on being your escort."

Ariana blushed. Silvan smiled—a protective smile that caused them both to duck their heads.

"I couldn't just leave her to your devices, Gwen." He clapped his hands on the table and leaned toward Gwendolyn. "You would have just been all mysterious to her until she was so confused she wouldn't know which way to turn!"

"Take care to remember who raised you, young man!" The woman tilted her head at a comical angle and raised an incredulous eyebrow. "I've still the spunk to spank those who would be most embarrassed by it, especially now."

They spoke with such mirth and affection toward each other. Ariana must have been looking at them perplexed, for Gwendolyn spoke up.

"Silvan's dear mother died in childbirth, and his father from grief, so I raised him here on this mountain as my own child." Gwendolyn swung her arm in a grand gesture. "And now he won't go away!"

"So you're family, too?" Ariana asked, her heart aflutter. "A cousin, perhaps?"

"Same race only, Lady Ariana. And not exactly family... yet!"

*   *   *

Gwendolyn stifled a chuckle with a cough. Silvan decided to claim his promised role along with a more, ah, personal role toward Ariana. She had enough to deal with, an unfamiliar culture as well as a new home and heavy revelations of fate. Before any of the important stuff comes out, the only boy she's met of her own race has decided to *flirt* her to death! Gwendolyn smiled at

Ariana's red face. And yet, who better to get her used to this life than someone close to her age who could teach her all the simple facts that were common knowledge to all who lived on these mountains.

Thankfully, the food arrived and broke the awkwardness of teenage discomfort. Men and women as fascinating as what they carried brought out platter upon platter of healthful foods, prepared to perfection. Ariana noticed an absence of meat in the offerings. Either this house or this culture didn't eat meat for some reason. She felt relieved. *Never liked the stuff anyway.* She made a mental note to ask about it later.

Bright clothes billowed behind the waiters as they hurried for more. Bright eyes settled on Ariana briefly and then danced away. She cast shy smiles at them. The three ate together, Ariana eating as quickly as she politely could, Silvan eating as much as he politely could, and Gwendolyn dining delicately. Ariana caught Gwendolyn smiling at her, then she glanced away.

"Don't be shy, my dear. I just noticed you were half-starved," Gwendolyn waved her hand at Ariana's escort, "but you still can't out-eat Silvan!"

Ariana glanced at Silvan, hands and mouth smeared with food—and shared a small smile with Gwendolyn. Food beckoned her again, and she ate with more gusto. He offered a half-hearted sneer and continued eating.

Later, when all were sated with good food, Gwendolyn led them into a huge library and seated them around the hearth fire in large dark chairs. Ariana focused on a stack of books that lay on a table at Gwendolyn's side, with writing in several different languages, including her native English. Silvan sat where he could watch Ariana's face. He already knew what she would learn and said he wanted to gauge her reaction. Gwendolyn pressed her fingers together, her elbows on either side supported by the chair arms.

"Tell me about your dreams, dear Ariana, and your nightmares as well."

"Well...I...sometimes I would have really good dreams, about running and dancing with my mother. All sorts of animals would come to play with us." Ariana ducked her head in embarrassment.

"There's no shame in happy dreams, Ariana." Gwendolyn encouraged her with a nod. "What sorts of animals?"

"Pretty horses and mythical ones, like centaurs and winged horses and unicorns, plus a griffin once. And others I didn't recognize. They were good dreams." Her eyes glazed over.

"Okay, and now your nightmares." Gwendolyn stared into the fire.

"Dragons and snakes and all things vile try to hurt me." She gulped. "Usually when my 'condition' was really painful. Huge snakes would try to crush me and dragons would try to talk to me, then eat me alive." Ariana shuddered. "I always woke up at the right time, right before... except the last time, when I couldn't wake up. Or I *thought* I was still asleep. But I couldn't dream with my eyes open, could I? It hurt so badly!"

Gwendolyn nodded at Silvan, whose face was anxious. He grasped Ariana's arm and took her hand. Ariana's eyes widened and she looked at him anew.

"It was the night my parents died, when my *condition* turned into something more deadly." She clung to Silvan's hand.

Gwendolyn nodded, deep in thought. "I promised I would explain your 'condition,' and the resulting occurrence." Gwendolyn lifted a thick book and thumbed through the first few pages. "But first I want to ask you something."

Ariana leaned in expectantly.

"What if I were to tell you that your life up to this point has happened in exactly the way it was supposed to? That every moment from here on out is also guided by a higher power?"

"I would say that I know God has power in our lives." Ariana nodded, her stomach churning. *It was hard to believe before, but I know what I know.* "God moves like love moves, my mother once said."

"But, for you, it is something much more. Your path, your gift, is beyond imagination. And only you can accomplish it."

Ariana sighed. "So I've been told. But I guess if anything can make me believe, it would be this." She stroked the scar on her forehead.

Gwendolyn gave her an odd look. Then she smiled and waited. A log crashed in the fire and sent sparks upward. Ariana watched the embers float and fade, dying into ash on the hearth. Then she returned her eyes to Gwendolyn.

"Do you believe in a higher power?" Gwendolyn asked, her tone gentle. "In God? In Yahweh or another entity?"

"Yes," Ariana replied. "I believe lots of them exist out there, since there's biblical context for it, and no proof to the contrary. But Yahweh is my higher power. I don't always agree with him, but I'm not perfect," she said with a shrug.

"Do you understand predestination?"

"Oh, I understand it," she answered Gwendolyn with an earnest smile, but this line of conversation tugged at her memory with an odd sense of familiarity. "Maybe I'm just resistant to those teachings! I just don't believe in destiny that's set in stone like that. I also don't believe I exercise blind faith in the Creator, which may be a problem to some believers. Prophecy and destiny are never that simple, and never without casualties."

"I see," Gwendolyn replied, a shadow of sorrow in her face. "That is a strong stance to take in some circles, but we welcome your take on it, Ariana. If destiny doesn't guide us, what is our purpose as believers?"

"To believe," she answered simply, nodding to the books on the table, one of which she recognized as the Holy Bible. "Believing deeply guides our actions. Not believing deeply also guides our actions. The only thing that changes is what structures our belief, since everyone believes in something." She gazed into the fire for a long moment, structuring her reply carefully, taking courage in Gwendolyn's welcome gesture to continue.

"One could argue that if we are given a purpose to fulfill and we ignore it, Yahweh will strip us of that destiny and give it to another." Ariana gestured from one extreme to the next, her hands blocking the firelight and casting shadows on her face. Still, her belly fluttered nervously with the conversation. "If we have a talent and don't use it for him, he will not prosper that talent. Destiny that is transferable isn't destiny. That would make fate a fickle thing. Free will is grounded in the fact that the Creator made us, knows the outcome, but offers anyway. Allows us to stumble when we pull stuff into our path with bad decisions."

"Why does God allow suffering and cause the bad things to happen?" Gwendolyn asked.

For the first time since her arrival, Ariana's words came out strong and unwavering. "He doesn't *cause* the bad things in life. I admit that I try to blame him for taking my parents sometimes, but again, I'm not perfect. He can help us to see the bad things in a different light that makes us stronger. He can lay out a path for us using those strengths, but we still have to choose to take it."

Gwendolyn's smile widened. "I hear your mother in your words! The same fire of spirit! She was strongest in her faith."

"She taught me everything but this," Ariana gestures around the room to indicate her new secret family in a mountain carved into a house. "And I'm happy to discuss faith. It brings me closer to *her,* as much as the Creator, I think. But I don't understand how my faith affects my condition." Ariana stared past Gwendolyn into the flames, taking comfort in the dancing orange and yellow light. "Faith is spiritual, mental and emotional, not physical."

"Your faith is part of your purpose. Your purpose is rooted in the genetics that led to your condition." Gwendolyn gestured beyond them into the fire. "Just as fire consumes wood to live and grow, the spirit consumes infirmity, pain and hard-learned lessons to get stronger. We grow beyond our limits, just as you survived beyond your condition."

"Purpose is a little easier to swallow than destiny. More action-oriented, I guess. But the spirit grows tired sometimes, overfed and lethargic on vast suffering," Ariana whispered with a quivering smile, shaking her head a little to rid herself of that omnipresent picture of her parents dead in the floor beside her bed. "Believing is work, with a defined purpose or not, I suppose."

"What of those who do not believe?" Gwendolyn looked at her book. "In God, in any higher power? What of those who cannot see the science in intelligent design?"

"Everyone believes in something. In a god or gods, in science, in nature." Ariana furrowed her brow, dismissing the question with a wave of her hand. "I said that already. Share our heart if they ask, receive if they offer. And we are to love others, not judge. That's the Creator's job, not mine."

"What power do we wield as believers?"

"Dominion over all the earth and all creatures. Destruction of spiritual darkness and the evil that lives within it." Ariana gasped in realization. "She meant that literally, didn't she? Not just in some idealistic, internal, metaphysical, spirit-driven way?"

Gwendolyn laughed. "Exactly. And you have already fought once, subconsciously." She clapped her hands on her thighs. "Sounds like you are well-trained."

"Does that mean my purpose is to literally fight evil?" Ariana asked, incredulous. "Like the monster that attacked me, if it was even real?"

"Looks like that might be the case," Gwendolyn answered. "And that creature, that spiritual monster, was real, and an extension of our enemy—of an enemy we have struggled against since time immemorial."

"Oh," she replied, her voice growing quiet with resolve, and a hint of vengeful, righteous anger. "There's more where that thing came from? And my purpose is to destroy it?"

She clenched her free hand into a fist and squeezed the hand that Silvan offered. "Well, I am nothing if not a fighter," she whispered, casting a determined, vicious smile toward Gwendolyn and standing, bathed in firelight. "I'll be your Purposed One. If Mother was an Angel of Peace in Father's eyes, I'll be an avenging one in the eyes of the Creator himself."

The peaceful crackling of a cozy library's fire went on as Ariana's voice boomed across the large room. Gwendolyn dabbed at the corner of her eye, a grateful smile on her lips. Ariana's parents had chosen to teach her after all. They didn't keep her in the dark about the Truth of the Spirit. The enemy eventually found her *because* she knew. Had she remained ignorant, her life would've been easier. Celeste knew this, but made her choice—perhaps the best choice in the end. Silvan stared, flabbergasted by the whirlwind conversation and the conviction of Ariana's words.

"They wanted to protect you! Why would they teach you the truth?" Silvan clenched her hand again. "The enemy would not have found you, wouldn't have fought you if you didn't know!"

"No, Silvan. Ariana's parents protected her *because* they taught her the truth. They couldn't leave her defenseless. They simply kept her safe as long as they could." Gwendolyn leaned forward, her fingertips pressed together. She had a distant look in her eyes.

"They knew she would fight when she was strong enough."

Tears streamed down Ariana's face. She felt the pressure of Silvan's fingers on her hand. "The more you know, the more you are responsible for. The greater the gift, the greater the *sacrifice*." She paused, her voice cracking as the faces of her parents flooded her sight. She shook her head in wonder. "They were preparing me my entire life!"

Gwendolyn nodded, tears still threatening to spill down her face. "Their sacrifice preserved your life." The flames danced in her blue eyes. "Now you know that destiny doesn't exist. Divine purpose does. You've chosen to fulfill that purpose?"

Ariana nodded, her jaw set in grim determination and a smoldering anger against this evil. She drew deep, cleansing breaths and carefully, deliberately suppressed the fire in her veins. She returned to her chair.

"Let's call your condition an overgrowth. We will call the event a defensive alicorn ejection." Gwendolyn peered into Ariana's eyes, gauging her reaction.

"Alicorn?" whispered Ariana, trying to place the word in her mental dictionary.

"That is the name of the coating on our bones." Gwendolyn turned her hands over in the firelight, staring at the fine bones and long fingers.

"I've heard of that word somewhere before. Now, to remember it..." Ariana furrowed her brow. "From some fantasy book I read about a unicorn? That's what I told you the spikes looked like."

Gwendolyn's lips twitched with a smile. Then she leveled Ariana with her gaze. "The alicorn overgrowth formed spikes that left your body at a high rate of speed to ease the tension of your overgrowth. And your enemy—the serpent that attacked you—triggered your body's natural defense." Gwendolyn gave her a moment to absorb that knowledge.

"I killed *it*, too?" Ariana stared at her hands. *And my parents.* "The blood was here. It was everywhere. But they couldn't see it. They thought I was talking about my blood, like I had lost my mind!"

"What you saw was real. Its blood on your body was real." Gwendolyn sighed. "It's unlikely that you killed the true enemy, though. But it seems you drew first blood by killing his underling!"

Gwendolyn's triumphant smile glowed in the firelight. Then Ariana shivered despite the heat. She dropped her head.

"The things you experience won't always be scary." Silvan leaned over and put a protective arm around her shoulders. "There will be happy times as well."

Ariana flinched. "I'm sorry. I'm angry at what happened. And scared of what *will* happen. I...I don't even know who I am anymore!"

"A brief history, then." Gwendolyn slid forward and leaned in candidly, her face resting on her graceful hands. "Centuries ago, our people lived far away from these mountains, on a great island in the center of the Atlantic Sea. We developed technologies so advanced that even our physical bodies evolved transcendent abilities! We were in peace, and happy. Then a great evil appeared in our world, devastating everything in its way, in search of a threat to its existence. Our knowledge and technology were less of a threat than the secret to our great peace. The enemy wished the whole world to fight. A great battle ensued." Gwendolyn's eyes grew distant, as if seeing the events from so long ago. "The evil was destroyed." She pressed her fingers to her temples. "But the ocean swallowed our entire homeland."

"A city swallowed by the ocean?" Ariana stared at Gwendolyn's interlaced fingers. "Like Atlantis?"

"Atlantis." Gwendolyn smiled. "Another name that shifted into legend after Plato wrote about us. He told it wrong, though, in favor of making his point." She chuckled.

"You mean to tell me that I'm from Atlantis?"

"Indirectly, yes." Gwendolyn produced a thick ancient volume from her table and opened it to a large hand-drawn map. "This is the account of our race, inscribed and copied throughout the ages. Kept secret from the world." She laid the book in Ariana's lap.

Ariana wiped nervous sweat from her hand and touched the worn, yellowed edges of the paper. She traced a finger around the gilded image and gently, holding her breath, turned the leaf to a finely crafted page of script. "This is like the old Bible illuminations!"

Gwendolyn returned to her seat without a sound. "There are two races who lived in harmony on Atlantis. One is indigenous, the race of Alcourne. Our people. The second is the humans, whom we brought to Atlantis to share our wealth of knowledge with the rest of humanity. But when the battle entered its final stage, the remaining humans scattered all throughout the rest of the world, carrying with them what little information they could salvage, leaving the few Alcourne who remained to fend for themselves."

A sheaf of onion-skin thin papers fluttered to the floor as Ariana turned another gold-leafed page. "What's this?" She gathered the scattered sheets carefully and stacked them. "Aristotle, Plato, Socrates, Leonardo da Vinci, Galileo. These are some of the greatest minds in history!" Ariana dragged her finger down a list of names on a transparent leaf.

"Contributors, all." Gwendolyn took the papers from Ariana. "Representing original human thought added to our collective wisdom."

"You said they ran away?" Ariana frowned. *But they were such formidable intellects!*

"They weren't soldiers." Gwendolyn dismissed their fleeing with a shrug. "We fled, too, in the end. There was so much death. Too much." The woman's tears welled up as if she had witnessed it all firsthand. "We fled to the mainland. We built great secret homes in the mountains and lived quietly in the forests there, using our salvaged technology to shield our presence and continuing our frantic research to regain what we had lost."

Gwendolyn paused for a long moment. Ariana wondered if the woman could have really been there. "We expected the enemy to destroy everything all over again. But it wasn't the enemy who discovered us. It was the humans. They thought we possessed something of importance to them, and we did. So our one-time companions hunted us like beasts to near extinction."

"That's horrible! They hunted you?" Ariana leaned forward in her seat, horrified. "Why?"

"The hunters were not to blame, my dear," Gwendolyn replied in response to Ariana's accusing eyes. "They had never known about Atlantis. The greedy guts—our former cohorts—who told them about us left out the part about our sentience." Gwendolyn's bitter smile glinted in the firelight. "And that lot never found our hiding places, never got more than our alicorn."

Ariana's face held an odd combination of sorrow and puzzlement. "But you fled, defeated? I thought you said the evil was destroyed?"

"The battle raged for years and years, you see. Being at peace did not mean we were without defenders." Smiling, Gwendolyn slipped from her chair and stood next to Ariana. She flipped through the ancient pages. She paused on a glorious two-page illumination detailing an epic battle against a dark enemy. "These are our greatest warriors."

Ariana gasped. "They're unicorns?" She traced a golden line down the beautiful creature's flank. Thick muscles and heavy feathered feet and a long spiraling horn—the creatures larger and less delicate than her picture books—could easily rip a tree from its roots. She turned to Silvan, wondering if he'd seen the lovely pictures in the book. The look on his face pleaded with her to understand.

"Yes, *we* are," said Silvan, his cheeks blazing. He stared into her eyes with such intensity that she looked away.

We are. Ariana's mind drew a blank. Alicorn, Unicorns, Atlantis. Evil. Divine Purpose. *We are what?* Then her jaw dropped. "I'm a freakin' unicorn?!"

Gwendolyn muffled a cackle with all the grace she could muster. She curled up like a child in her chair and had a good, hearty, contagious laugh. She beat on the arm of the chair. Tears rolled down her cheeks. After her initial shock of seeing the woman behave in such a manner, Ariana giggled along. She looked at Silvan, who was red-faced with embarrassment. He smiled and scratched his scalp.

Wiping tears away with the back of her frail-looking hand, Gwendolyn huffed and gasped to regain her composure. "How much do you know about genetics?"

Ariana smiled, not sure she was ready to believe that she was a unicorn and certain that this was some joke to lighten the mood. Ariana shrugged.

Gwendolyn sighed, shaking her head. "We focused all our research on a new problem. We had to protect our bloodline from dying off forever. So we decided to change our appearance. The great remaining Alcourne minds of Atlantis produced one final genetic code and spliced it into three Alcourne infants from particularly influential bloodlines. After days of agony, only one child survived the ordeal. Testing revealed that the code blended with her DNA perfectly, allowing the child to change her physical form at will. After attempting several forms, she settled on the shape of a human, the most logical form that would ensure our safety." Gwendolyn stared into the fire, then down at her hands. She shivered. "And try as she might, she could not return to her original form. She felt trapped in that mortal body, feeling it die with every breath."

The way Gwendolyn stared at her hands, Ariana believed all at once. No one said something like that and meant it so completely unless they *knew*. Her heart fluttered. "So I really am a unicorn? We really are from Atlantis. And you? You're that first one who changed shape?"

Gwendolyn's wide eyes answered her. "Using my pure blood, we generated and duplicated a genetic serum that was implanted into nearly every living Alcourne, forcing us all into human form."

Slack-jawed, Silvan stared at Gwendolyn. "It is true, then?"

"Everyone of any age tells those stories," she replied with a wave of her hand. "And only this one figured it out for sure!" But she bowed her head. "I'm sorry. I was bound by oath to never admit the truth unless I stood before the Purposed One." She nodded toward Ariana. "The old ones said that somewhere in that code lies all the knowledge and technology of Atlantis, as well as the secret to peace. And for the rare descendant, the code contains an open pathway to attaining our original form. I knew I'd lose them all over again, if the enemy found out that our precious secrets flow through our veins! And..." She glanced up, her lower lip quivering. "I felt like I lied to you all these years."

"Are you kidding?" Silvan wiped a tear and laughed. He scrambled over to hug her tightly. "Don't apologize! That's awesome! And you're amazing, saving so many of us!"

"So you forgive me for deceiving you?" Gwendolyn snuffled into Silvan's shirt.

"Of course," Silvan said in his softest voice. "Always. Besides..." He hugged her to his chest. "You're my family. And now, I know how *old* you really are!"

"Silvan Alcourne, you scoundrel!"

Gwendolyn playfully slapped his back. He

scurried away. The mood of the conversation lightened with Silvan's particular brand of death-defiance.

"After the change, we could work toward our collective purpose. Some powers we kept, others we had to give up." Her eyes grew distant. "Our people watched reality slowly dissolve into legend, until only a very few believed we ever existed. That is how we survived, at that cost."

"We were written into storybooks as metaphors for virility, but also purity and good against the most vile evil," Gwendolyn sighed, "when in reality that's not far from what we are."

Silvan took Ariana's hand as he returned to his seat. He smiled and spoke softly, "We still live in the forests. Nature thrives around us. They lost us beneath their very noses. We call ourselves Alcourne, a race name. A family name."

"When we transformed," Gwendolyn inspected her hands again, "we could no longer develop alicorn. A thin coat covers our bones and gives us some powers in healing and purifying. But we have to work hard to learn how to do these things."

Ariana looked at her hands and elbows, at her knees through the split in her tan pants. The pink scars were all there, not fading with time but healed more clearly than before. Her hand went to her breast. "My mother... she really did heal my heart."

"Yes, Ariana. So that you could survive the next trial in your life. Your condition was really an overgrowth of alicorn that you were unable to redirect. And when it got too bad, it found its own exit." Gwendolyn gestured to Ariana's scars. "Since your body is free of the excess, you are now ready to learn how to control it as it reemerges. How to control it, and how to use it. You, Ariana, are the only one among your race who can *produce* the alicorn, and all its inherent powers of healing, purification, and if need be, destruction."

Silvan broke in, "But that means the evil can sense its purity, and may come for you, so you and all the rest of us have to be ready. We must train."

His words held a note of urgency. His green eyes were solemn and worried, far from the grinning youth she remembered from earlier.

"I have chosen to fight. I'll kill them all if I can, now that I know I can touch them." Ariana ran her fingers over the pink stars dotting her knuckles. "*If some sort of transcendent power has been granted to me beyond that. But what exactly am I preparing for?"*

"For a journey, child. All your life, you felt different. It wasn't merely the disabling pain that made you so. Every moment, every dream, every breath made you who you are." Gwendolyn took the huge book from Ariana and leafed through the thin pages. "You came here. Your parents could only protect you so long from the evil, and now it awakens once more. As we speak it gains power. Soon it will seek us out, to find you." She opened the book to another two-page spread of artwork. A huge creature born of darkness blotted out the sun. Golden streaks of sunlight poured from behind the hulking silhouette, alighting on a lone figure with long white hair, holding a slim sword. "We pray you can defeat it."

Ariana stared at the vibrant drawing for a long time, until her eyes stung. She stared at the little white figure with long wavy hair. *Is that me? Or is that the last Purposed One?* A tiny jewel in the sword hilt caught her eye. A ruby. She stared until the whole conversation reverberated in her skull, rattling her nerves until she was tempted to scream or break down laughing. She did neither in the end, and simply sank deeply into her chair, numbed into silence. All that remained at the forefront of her mind is...*I can destroy them.*

"Too much information too fast? I figured I'd do that. I'm terribly sorry." Gwendolyn took her hand and searched her eyes. "I will answer all the questions you have for me once you've slept. In the meantime, Silvan is right. Tomorrow, after you've allowed this to sink in, we will hold the welcome feast, if you're ready. Then we will begin your training, dear one. And Silvan, your sworn protector, will be there every step of the way." Gwendolyn set Ariana's hand in her lap and smiled at Silvan. "I do apologize if this is an inconvenience. He is quite adamant."

"I...yes...no inconvenience...but, it's an awful lot to take in!" Ariana's voice wavered. She had more wordless questions than answers swimming in her head. Her hands trembled in her lap. Tears welled in her eyes and dripped onto her hands. Silvan touched her shoulder. He looked into her bleary eyes and pulled Ariana to her feet, wrapping his long arms around her. She tucked her head against his slim chest as sobs wracked her body.

"I'm here. Everything will be okay, I promise," he whispered into her ear. Then he closed his eyes. Where their skin touched a dim glow emanated. He pushed the healing light beyond their skin to her heart, the heart her mother had touched. She felt his heartbeat with hers. She felt her heart slowly calm, falling into the same strong pulse as Silvan's. Her sobs stopped. Her tears stopped. Everything was peaceful within her.

When she looked up at Silvan, he smiled warmly down on her.

"Few have looked forward to your return as much as Silvan." Gwendolyn stood at the door, ready to leave. "Few have the will to protect you as steadfastly as he shall. And it's okay to be afraid."

"I wasn't crying because I'm afraid. I'm relieved." She placed her hands over her heart, longing for her parents' embrace, if only for a moment. "All this time, I felt helpless. Now, I know I can bring Hell to creatures who brought Hell to my life. I. Am. Relieved."

Both Gwendolyn and Silvan regarded her for a long moment, unsure how to respond. Silvan's eyes flashed with fierce pride. His lips turned up in a smirk. And his heart felt fit to burst.

"This is the fire we've been searching for, isn't it?"

"I believe so," Gwendolyn smiled, turned, and then continued out of the library.

"May I have one request before tomorrow?"

"Of course, my girl."

"I want to spend time with my parents."

"Silvan knows where their graves are." Gwendolyn leaned against the doorway, her voice heavy with a personal sorrow. "Seek and find your peace there, dear child."

*   *   *

Ariana and Silvan emerged into the cooling air. The sun cast violet shadows over the pastel garden and sank behind vast ranges of mountains and hills. The huge garden she thought she'd imagined bloomed with all the colors of spring, though spring had not yet arrived. She stared at the low rock walls and marble statues, all amid pillows and curtains of colorful foliage. Silvan led her through cool grass to a smooth dirt trail between the trees. Then she remembered her bare feet. She watched every step, worried about every forest warning she'd ever heard. She told Silvan and he smiled at her.

"I was serious. You don't need shoes." Silvan placed his hand behind her shoulder and gave her a gentle push. "The ground you tread is blessed, Ariana."

She stepped on a pebble and cried out, grabbing her foot. "This stupid blessed rock bruised my stupid blessed foot." She limped on ahead of him into the forest, grumbling to herself. "And are you always going to make comments like that?"

"As long as you keep blushing like that!" Silvan punctuated his grin with a light-hearted laugh.

"Hmph! Some protector you are!"

He laughed and rushed to catch up. "The pebbles fall outside by jurisdiction, dear Ariana."

He took her hand and guided her over fallen logs and up steep hills. Finally, an expanse of forest that was almost a clearing appeared before them. Soft moss and vines covered the trees. The ground was rich and dark—a deciduous forest floor. As far as she could see, narrow white and gray headstones arose from the heavy dirt and roots. No undergrowth sprouted here. The only trees seemed gracefully arched and cultivated. The heavy, still air and the strong scent of flowers filled her nose.

Farther back, the nature-battered stones stood three or four times farther apart than those down the slope. The older stones had simple, beautiful names but no dates. Doshonnen, Sylfan, Gratiara, Desul, Aryanna. She started at the name that looked like hers.

"Your name is there, too." She pointed in surprise. "Well, sort of."

"It is an honor to take the name of our ancestors. The slain were buried there, just before we chose to change shape." Silvan whispered, so as not to disturb the silence. "And here are the younger ones. Our lifespan shortened when we became humanoid, so we don't live much longer than them, now."

Ariana decided the dates must be etched in error. One of the younger deceased would have been over two hundred years old when he died! She turned to him in confusion, but he only nodded and spread his hands to indicate the newest additions. Ariana's heart sank when she saw freshly turned earth and new headstones. The tears fell freely; she didn't bother wiping them. Silvan led the short distance, keeping his lips pressed tight. Then he reached above them and took down from a bend in the branch a small pouch and rolls of pale, gauzy silk. These he placed in her hands.

"Her seeds are in the pouch. The silk covers the fresh dirt and the seeds." He gestured with his hands.

"It is our burial custom, to give a kind of life to the departed. It is also an honor to be laid here. Your father was once a human, and now is family to us all."

"I know *this*." She turned the little indigo pouch over in her hands. Silver and white embroidery and beading on one side sparkled, revealing a pair of angel wings. "My mother carried this with her all the time."

Silvan reached into his pocket and pulled out a similar green pouch. "We all carry one. The seeds are gathered from the graves of our parents." His voice cracked. "We keep them with us. Older Alcournes believe that we infuse the seeds with our power throughout our lives and it gives those plants special qualities."

"What do you believe?"

"I feel like I'm carrying the spirit of my mother," Silvan whispered.

Ariana stared at the bag for a long time, realizing she would carry her own little bag of seeds one day. She would always have a physical and spiritual connection with her parents, though they lay under the dirt at her feet. Despite the warm spring-like breeze, she shuddered. She poured the variety of seeds into her open palm. They felt oddly warm against her skin. She walked around the edge of both graves, casting the seeds across the dark earth. She placed the two larger seeds behind each headstone.

She knelt at the headstones, pulling the silk up to their bases. Then she knelt there behind the stones, a hand on each one as her tears flowed down the smooth stone. She mumbled to her parents and softly prayed to God for guidance.

When she opened her eyes, Silvan walked over and knelt at the foot of the graves. He gave thanks aloud for their sacrifice; he gave thanks for their daughter's life; he gave thanks for the love they had shown him when he was small. He also asked to help their daughter perform her last ceremony to them.

By then, Ariana had come to kneel quietly beside Silvan.

"I thought I would be more upset. I thought I would lose it again, but I don't think they want me to. I have a feeling that they want me to heal and to live." Tears spilled from her eyes.

"They do want you to live. And learn. And at the last, they willed you to fulfill your purpose. That's how much they loved you, enough to give all they had to let you continue on," he rasped. Tears sprang to his green eyes, too.

Ariana nodded. "Why do we really plant the seeds, Silvan? How long will it take them to grow?"

"We plant them as a living memorial to one who has lived among us. And they will grow by the power of our love for them, tonight. Our people have special energy circuits that flow in tune with nature. You need to learn how to manipulate that flow. Your first lesson starts now."

He took her hand in his and placed it flat on the silken cover. "Put your other hand at the other corner." He instructed her with clipped sadness in his voice as he did the same on the opposite side. "Now *show* them. Feel your love for your parents flow through you, like a fire beginning in your belly. Your love has the power to give life to their memory. Listen for the seedsong."

As he spoke, she felt a tingle in the hand that touched hers. A similar glow, of a more muted tone, emanated from his hand and spread to hers. His pale skin had a shimmering cast. The beginnings of a small smile alighted on his face.

She felt the warmth rise from her belly, from her healed heart and tingle all over her body, then slowly creep out of her hands. The glow disappeared a short distance from their fingers and appeared to sink. The air rang with a trilling vibrato as each seed called out to her from its resting place. She *knew* all at once how their roots sank and their greenery arose, how the light nourished them and how water made them strong. She knew how her strength could become theirs. A bug chirped far overhead, distracting Ariana. Then the seedsong faded from her ears.

Startled, Ariana opened her eyes to the rising darkness. She squeezed her eyes shut and tried to produce the warmth and light again, remembering the feeling and the tingling all over. She squeezed her eyes shut and pushed at the light as hard as she could. The seedsong drowned out all other sound. When she opened her eyes, Silvan stared at her with an odd expression in his emerald eyes. Then she noticed the brilliant glow beneath her hands—a glow that came from her body.

From beneath the silken cloth burst sprouts of green that were pale next to her bright light. Silvan looked into her eyes and smiled. Slowly, flowers bloomed over each grave, vivid yellows and purples and reds. From behind the bed of flowers, from behind each stone, rose a slender shoot covered in bark. Each sapling climbed upward with graceful speed, then bent to meet in the middle. The trunks twined around each other, creating a single tree between the stones. Roots anchored the stones in place and fenced the perimeter of the graves protectively.

Finally, the gracefully curving white trunk erupted in branches carrying every shade of pink flower that she could imagine. The tree was shaped like a mimosa, her mother's favorite tree, with pale green fronds of leaves, but the trunk was stark white. Staring at the tree, Ariana let the light fade from her hands. The delicate blossoms streamed through the evening air, creating a lovely shower of color in the darkened forest. The scent was so delicate and beautiful that Ariana closed her eyes to the beauty and breathed in the aroma.

Then other scents flooded the clearing, floating above the sweetness of the flowers. Her mother's perfume swirled around Ariana in a sudden breeze, followed immediately by the light cologne of her father. Celeste, the Angel, and her true love, Ariana's dark eyed father Jacob. Ariana felt the light breeze ruffling her hair, like her father always did. A sense of peace overwhelmed her. Tears streamed down her cheeks, each sparkling as it splattered on the rich dirt of her parents' graves.

Ariana felt some of her worry and pain drain through her knees into the dirt. She found her peace. She would find her new path. She looked at her companion. Silvan's wondering eyes widened. His face paled. With his free hand, he grabbed the hem of his shirt and breathed in deeply.

"I can smell her perfume! It's Celeste!" New tears flowed down his cheeks.

Ariana sniffed her sleeve, then a lock of her hair. The scent of her parents saturated her clothing and hair like no mere shampoo could. She grasped Silvan's hand and they both rose together. She looked around at the peaceful garden and sighed. She pulled him toward the path until he stumbled to catch up. Silvan squeezed her hand more tightly than necessary.

Looking up into his emerald eyes, she saw gleaming tears that he blinked back. Worry, always present, nestled deep within, called out to her. But what is he worried about now? Ariana shook her head, confusing him even more. *Nothing. My parents are at rest. We're all safe, for the moment.* His eyes beckoned her heart into a faster beat. *Unless he's worried about me.* She shook her head again.

"Why do you keep shaking your head?" Silvan's throat was tight with emotion. "I haven't even said anything!"

"I'm answering myself, not you." Ariana tossed her wrist in a flippant wave.

"Not nearly enough of an answer." He bent to kiss her hand. "My Lady Ariana."

"It'll have to do, for now." Ariana curtsied despite the hotness of her cheeks. *My sworn protector.* She shook her head again. She couldn't say something like that aloud!

"For now, then." Silvan smiled down at her again. "That light, by the way, was amazing! And for a first time out! Pretty impressive. The brightest I've ever seen. And to grow even the headstone trees in one push. Most folks have to visit daily for months to grow all that! Proof enough of your blood for my purposes."

She shrugged off asking about his purposes. "It was the most peaceful I've felt in a long time." Ariana closed her eyes, hearing the seedsong again. Feeling the warmth of Silvan's hand and the glow of his green eyes in her light, she sighed. "Was my light really so bright?"

Silvan flipped over her hand and traced the veins on her pale wrist. "We communicate with things through the energy flowing through our blood. Where blood is close to the surface, energy can be transmitted. But we can only transmit a small portion of what we possess, above and beyond what we need to live. Everyone has a limit to how hard they can push, possibly except you."

"So could I push too hard and die in training?"

Her matter-of-fact question caught Silvan's worried look again. "We don't know. Possibly. So we need to teach you to limit yourself."

"I suppose I must sleep soon, since tomorrow's going to be such a tough experience in training." She paused, suddenly exhausted, as they emerged from the forest into the garden. "Wow! That was a quick return!" Turning to him, she whispered, "Thank you so much for everything, Silvan."

"That smile is payment enough for me." He grinned.

She threw her arms around him in gratitude. He hugged her back for a long time. When she pried his arms from around her, she smiled at him, feeling the light flowing behind her features. *I will be powerful! And strong. And skilled. Then I will fulfill my purpose, and protect everyone from this nasty evil thing that hunts me!* She nodded and headed toward the mansion.

"I wish you'd stop answering yourself like that," Silvan muttered as he trotted up behind her.

Back in the mansion, Ariana dredged up an uncomfortable piece of information everyone had glanced over. "What are these 'Welcome Banquets' like?"

Silvan thought for a moment, a finger on his bottom lip. "Well, I have to dress up and stand straight and behave," he began, "but I can eat until I'm sick and no one will stop me as long as Gwendolyn doesn't say that I'm 'showing myself'."

"I see." Ariana giggled. "Very... mature."

"I see a lot of folks I don't know all that well. I bet every Alcourne will come to this one!"

"Oh, my!" Ariana felt woozy.

"Gwen's awesome, though. She remembers everyone's name and family for generations. They call her Matron or Matriarch because she's the oldest they know. Little do they know about her real age!" He cast a mischievous smirk regarding their private joke.

Ariana frowned. No one really would believe that she's the first, anyway. But the rush of information swirled around her head yet again.

"Oh! You're the guest of honor! You'll need an appropriate escort, ya know!" Silvan said, as if the thought just occurred to him. "Someone to protect you from too much, uh, badgering!"

"Hmmm?" Ariana said, losing track of her contemplation. "Is that a date request? Or an order?"

"Which would be more effective?"

"Probably the date." Ariana blinked, thinking hard. "I've never had one."

"Me neither."

"No way! You're way too..." Ariana clamped her mouth shut, her face blazing hot. She had reached the door to her room and her hand was on the knob. In her head, she started with letter A and had trouble stopping. Amazing, attractive, beautiful, charismatic...

"Way too what, Lady Ariana?" he said with a grin.

"Way too old!" She opened and closed her mouth, blinking up at him. "Good night, Silvan!"

"Good night, my Lady," he said as he pulled her hand to his mouth.

She pulled it away as his lips brushed her palm. She ran into her room. She settled onto her bed sometime later, her heart still fluttering from Silvan's touch.

*   *   *

Silvan couldn't wipe the goofy smile off his face. His heart was light as he rounded the corner to his bedroom. His door was ajar. He pushed it open and found a scripted scrap of paper on his table with the words written in a finely honed handwriting he knew was Aunt Gwen's: *Is she a dancer? When she's ready, then so must you be!*

He was puzzled at the words until he looked up at his closet door. His shoulders slumped. On the back of the door, Gwendolyn had hung a finely tailored ensemble in shades of black and gray. He sighed at the strangling neckpiece and difficult lacey cuffs and stifling warm cloth. He felt once more like he was dressing for the wrong century. In a place where he never wore shoes, he was required to don evening wear. He turned the note over in his hands. There was a scribble on the back: *If you hurry, you'll have a say in what dress Ariana wears from the Wardrobe.* The note fluttered to the floor as Silvan's door swung open again and he was gone.

5: WELCOME

Ariana clung to Silvan's arm, terrified of the thousand guests and their thunderous applause. Her heart pounded in her ears, but even the rush of blood couldn't drown out the sound. Her fingers, by nervous habit, traced the edges of the starburst scar right above her brows. She only walked out the door! She had done nothing special, nothing supporting any great purpose, yet. She cowered beneath their gaze, trembled with each wave of their joyful voices.

Silvan paused and whispered in her ear, "Is it too soon? Do you want to go back?" His grip tightened on her fingers, prying them loose from his elbow. She shook her head and continued forward at his urging, her blue gossamer skirt billowing in the warm spring breeze. She couldn't very well run away, could she?

The lavish courtyard dripped with glowing lights and cascading flowers. The carved tables drooped under their burden of food and drink. She glanced at her dress, a gauzy bit of finery that Silvan fawned over from the moment he saw it. She smoothed her long hair back under its wreath of cut flowers. Gwendolyn must have spent so much time and money on the event! Though scared witless, Ariana couldn't bear to disappoint her aunt.

As if sensing her worry and distress, the guests tapered off their applause. Soon, the atmosphere took on a much calmer tone as lilting conversation filled the courtyard. Ariana sought out familiar faces among those she had met.

Across the sea of pale, gleaming faces and flowing hair, Gwendolyn ushered in and greeted even more guests at the metal gate. The press of bodies suffocated Ariana to the point of collapse. However, seeing Gwendolyn behave with such grace shamed Ariana. She had been taught better manners! *I'll have to find something positive.* Seeing how closely the group huddled, she knew one thing for sure. There would be no room to dance for those who could dance! The butterflies left her stomach. Ariana heaved a sigh of relief.

Silvan leaned in. "Sighs consume the heart's blood. Are you okay?"

Ariana smiled for the first time that day. "Yes. I just realized I won't have to dance!"

He faltered in his step, looking into the distance. "You don't want to dance with me?"

"Silvan," she began, "I...We...It's not that."

When he didn't say anything, she dug in her heels and forced him to look at her. She gazed into the emerald depths of his eyes, knowing she had hurt him deeply. But just because of dancing? She didn't understand why dancing was so important to him! Then her heart fell into her belly and she knew why she was relieved.

"It's because I...feel guilty," Ariana whispered. "I don't want to dance if Mother can't dance with me, like we did when I was small."

"But she saved you."

"Yes," Ariana answered.

"And she taught you how to dance?"

"Yes," Ariana replied, eyeing him suspiciously. "But it's been years!"

"Dancing made her happy?"

"Yes." Her heart pounded. She knew Silvan would win this battle.

"Then let us all make her happy. We'll all dance for her!"

Silvan took her hand and led her to the center of the courtyard, where paving stones spiraled into a wide circle. He held her close, swaying back and forth for what felt like an eternity to Ariana. She heard his steady breathing, felt his heartbeat beneath her fingers, and closed out the terrifying press of people—Ariana's people—until all else faded away.

Then Silvan took her hand and spun her out from his body. Her feet moved of their own accord, remembering the grace of her distant childhood. Ariana kept her eyes closed, for once fully trusting Silvan and knowing that one peek at those around her would crumple her resolve. *Yes, I'll dance for you, Mother!* Tears arose in her closed eyes and trickled down her cheeks.

A solitary voice rose above the crowd, singing an enchanting elegy to the night. Others joined in, providing harmony and counterpoint, while others took up instruments, all among rhythmic clapping. Pipes and strings shook loose the last of Ariana's fear and apprehension. She whirled in Silvan's strong and surprisingly capable embrace. She spun and stepped and swayed away her sorrow, at last shedding tears of joy as her heart—the heart her parents healed—soared above the loving and welcoming throng of Ariana's newfound family.

When finally the music died down and Ariana reluctantly opened her eyes, she looked up into the emerald eyes of Silvan. Only Silvan remained out of the whole world, at least for a long moment. She tried with all her might to show him her heart with just that one stare, to let him know her gratitude for proving that she must dance, and for being a rock upon which she could place her trust. He smiled, a goofy expression—all transparent and no shadows. She liked his smile.

Then a hand clapped Silvan roughly on the shoulder, the owner congratulating him on such dainty steps for a man. Another man chided him for his shoddy footwork and ruffled his hair. Silvan took the jibing well, but then they dragged him away.

Ariana turned all around in the center of the circle, looking again for a familiar face, a note of panic in her heart. Young men and women ringed the circle, waiting their turn to dance. Some of the younger girls stared at Ariana with haughty glances full of jealousy. Ariana felt nervous until she caught them leering at Silvan. She blinked in confusion. *He does have others who are interested!* She smiled politely at the girls and executed her best curtsy.

Then a young man with short white hair introduced himself as Leif, gave an elegant bow, and asked her to dance. She politely accepted, though she knew who would receive the last dance of the evening. Ariana sought out Silvan, who eyed her possessively, even though he stood in a small sea of beautiful lady suitors. She smiled at him and allowed Leif to whirl her around to a more upbeat tune.

Ariana lost the hours of the evening to dancing and greeting and struggling to learn names and locations and other fundamentals of the Alcourne race. As the evening drew to a close, sure as the sunset, Silvan found her for the final dance. The last song of the evening lingered on the breeze, ebbing and flowing with the sounds of tree frogs and crickets.

Her heart full of contentment, Ariana leaned against Silvan's slim, solid chest. He smelled of honeysuckle and a half-dozen perfumes from the other girls who had stolen his dances all evening. Ariana chuckled at the thought, amazed that he had given them nothing of himself in so many years.

"What's funny?" he asked. His voice was soft and just for her.

She shook her head. "You spent your life dedicated to me, and I didn't even know you." Ariana smiled. "You could've started a family, lived a little. But you still waited. How did you know I'd even come back?"

Silvan pressed his lips against her hair, swaying to the music for a long time. When Ariana started to regret her question, Silvan answered. "Because I believe that everyone has half a soul. One half that fits perfectly with another half, like a puzzle. When we're truly blessed, we find our other half. When we aren't, we settle for another half. We may be happy, but we're just incomplete. Or we don't settle, and choose solitude. There has never been another half that fits like you since the day I first saw you."

"But I was just a baby," Ariana said. "You couldn't know, could you?"

"I think part of me knew from the day you were born," Silvan replied. "So I made the promise. Some of us are special like that, with knowing things." He looked down at her confused face. Then he stroked her cheek with his long, thin fingers.

"But what if I'm just normal, nothing special after all?"

"You're perfect for me, Purposed or not."

Ariana sank against Silvan again, stymied by his confession and unsure of how to respond. She clung to his shirt as the last music trailed off on the springtime breeze.

6: THE JEWELRY BOX

Ariana gazed across the tops of mountains from her perch in the bend of a branch thirty feet in the air. A bitter breeze caught waves of her long white hair and whipped it behind her head. Her pale face tilted to the side, a frown sending thin furrows across her scarred brow. She listened hard for a sound that human ears could not detect. Heavy pale lashes hung over soft pink eyes half closed in concentration. All of nature's chittering faded in her silent focus.

At fourteen years old, Ariana lost all that mattered to her—her parents, home and life. Four years of her new life and family, new friends and home, had filled her heart to the brim. Silvan's training was grueling on her worst days and thrilling on her best days. She strengthened her body and learned how to fight. She learned to focus the inherent powers of her race. She healed fast when bruised or cut and ran faster than even the other Alcournes. To top it off, she was gifted with longer lifespan than normal humans, if she got the chance to die of natural causes. Her heart still pounded at the loss of her parents. *But they're right here in my heart!* Each day among her people had been a fonder blessing than the day before, filled with new family and new people to love.

The faintest crack of a small twig reached her ears. She couldn't afford to sink into the past. Ariana leaned into the open air from her perch. He hunted her.

Her senses heightened. He had arrived below, upwind and to her right. He hadn't found her yet. She descended the tree lithely and stepped off the path into the brush. Her feet made no sound as she trod through the forest that winter had not touched, even far into January. An evening chill crept through the trees. Shadows loomed beneath the leafy canopy. Only the habitation of the Alcournes staved off much of the damage from winter. Snow had fallen, yet the pulsating energy of Ariana's brethren helped life flourish in the surrounding forests. The lush foliage blocked light from Ariana's searching eyes. Several moments of intense silence began to scare her, for all her expertise and training. She moved deeper into the stillness despite her fear, skirting a path that led somewhere she often visited. Keeping trees to her back and senses peaked, she made her way toward the burial ground of her ancestors and her parents. *Why would he hunt all the way out there?*

An overwhelming vision froze her steps and flooded her mind: death and a serpent and thousands of silhouetted creatures stood on dark foreign soil, waiting to die. *I know this place.* Ariana reached out her hand into the landscape. *But why?* Her hand flickered in her sight. *I've never been, but it's within reach!* The sky roared above her. She clamped her hands to her ears and ducked. A huge dragon wheeled within an inch of her head and then pumped its mighty wings to soar above the smoke that filled the sky. Ariana heard, "Stand up!" and obeyed. A young girl with fiery hair stood before her. The girl spoke a name—Taiyo—and then disappeared into the wilderness. A flash of silver in the form of another person caught Ariana's eye, then was gone, whisked away in turmoil and darkness. Then her vision cleared and the path to the gravesites wavered before her once again. She stared at her trembling white hands and the pink stars that scarred her knuckles. More frequent, more disturbing, clearer and urgent—the visions left her quaking in fear.

As she took her next step, the air at her back parted for a new form that landed silently inches behind her. *He found me!* She was not fast enough to evade him; disoriented, her fear and confusion over the vision still lingered. Strong arms wrapped around her and tightened their grasp. The suffocating arms became coils of a large snake in her mind. In a flash, Ariana caught her breath and pushed alicorn down the shafts of her forearm bones and sent a spear from each elbow. Her blood sprayed. She felt it trickle down to her wrist.

Her captor released her and instinct drove her to swing her deadly right elbow for the attacker's head. Her blow missed and sank into a tree trunk instead, burying the sharp shaft of alicorn inches deep. Ariana twisted the joint and broke off the alicorn. She grasped the end of her spear, pulling it from the tree.

She spun on her enemy, wary of his next movement. Her spiral weapon stabbed out like a knife and caught metal in a dull clang. Her left elbow spun before her to block a return attack. The next second, he pinned her wrists and pushed her gently against the tree. She stared into her captor's eyes in fright.

"I'm glad I can still dodge quicker than you can attack, my dear sweet Ariana." Silvan's deep voice held a playful tone.

Her clarity returned. "Oh, I didn't hurt you, did I?" She rubbed her wrists when he released them.

"Only my ego, dear one." That grin melted her heart. "I expected to catch you on guard, rather than off. That defensive mechanism can be, ah, dangerous at times."

"I had a vision again. A dragon, in a place I know but don't." She pursed her lips, realizing how odd that sounded when spoken aloud. "A little girl with fiery hair spoke to me, too. But the dragon!"

"Sounds like you have an earful for Gwendolyn." Silvan scratched his head. "I'm afraid I'm not much help."

"It's not your fault." Ariana licked her thumb and rubbed the drying blood on her elbow, smearing it around more than cleaning it. "Besides, I could've hurt you!"

He reached for her elbow and pulled out a soft towel from his pack. He wiped at the closed wounds until the blood was gone and shoved the soiled cloth into his waistband. He kissed each closed star-wound lightly.

Ariana stared at his face, concentrating on the set of his strong, angular jaw. Silvan was taller than when she first met him, and much broader of shoulder. Leanly muscled and long-legged, he had become a strong, beautiful man with that same messy silver-gray hair and joyful green eyes.

"What was the dragon doing in your vision?"

Ariana sighed. "Diving at my head, trying to remove it from my shoulders."

Silvan blinked in shock, speechless. She smiled at him and relaxed against the tree. Ariana had grown, too—nearly a foot her first year without excess alicorn stunting her growth. She was an elegant five feet seven. She wore clothes that left her knees, elbows and shoulders open for her alicorn, having destroyed many of her older garments before she realized the necessity. She went barefoot with confidence now and let her white hair flow loosely down the length of her back. Her pale pink eyes held little of the gloom of loss they once held.

Silvan watched her eyes. She stared back into his with her heart fluttering. His manner became unsure and sheepish. *Totally unlike him*, Ariana thought.

"I wanted to ask you a very important question, Ariana." Silvan scratched his head again, looking everywhere but at her. "Remember when I told you that you're perfect for me, Purposed or not?"

"Is that your question?" Her cheeks blazed.

"No. I don't know how to ask it." He frowned and stared at the ground.

"Just ask it." Her embarrassment turned to irritation. *He never acts unsure of himself! What in the world could it be?* She opened her mouth to scold him for his suspicious behavior, but he shut her up with his mournful, terrified stare.

"Alright." Silvan took her hand. "I think you have the other half of my soul. Can you... do you... love me, too?" He dropped his head yet again, unable to keep his eyes locked on hers.

Ariana stood silent for a moment, blinking in confusion. Her heart pounded so hard it ached. She had just assumed he understood her all these years. That he was just performing a duty to her, even though she cared so deeply for him. She sought the words in her head for a long time, then struggled to wrap her lips around them.

"Since the first time you called me 'Lady' I knew I would love you." Ariana softened her words with a tender smile. "You...there's only ever been room for you in my heart. I don't know if it's fate or if I'm just a silly dreamer, but..." She held his hand against her cheek. "If I'm allowed to have a heart's desire, then it's you."

Tears fell unbridled from his bright eyes when she finished. He wrapped his arms around her shoulders and threatened to squeeze the life out of her. Resting his cheek on her head, he sighed. *How did I not know how he felt?* Silvan always flirted passively, just to make her blush—or so she thought. Gwendolyn said things that made Ariana wonder. He was always so kind. Wouldn't even strike her during training, though she begged him not to hold back for her sake.

"Am I that dense?" Ariana looked up at him, clearly perplexed. "I thought I just monopolized your time and leaned into a promise made when you were three years old!"

"What?" he mumbled into her hair.

"I mean, you all but said the words to me these last four years." Ariana pulled away from his embrace. She ticked off points on her fingers. "When you were of age, you avoided marrying into the other households. You ignore your persistent flock of lady suitors to the point of rudeness. They still bring you tokens of their affection and hang on your every word! I disappear until they're gone, because they already glare at me when your back is turned, like I've done something horrible in training with you. And you greet them formally enough, but it's like they're not even there."

Silvan's infectious laughter cut off her incredulous rambling. She stared at him in confusion. "No. You've just been very focused on your goal of destroying evil and such. Every step in my life has led toward you, Lady Ariana. I've saved every touch, every kiss for you."

His smiling lips kissed her face all over, the warmth of each touch sending a jolt of emotion into her heart. Silvan nuzzled her ear and pulled back to let his mouth meet hers. Tears still streaming, he kissed her, putting all his heart into exploring her lips. Tears sprang to Ariana's eyes, too, when Silvan leaned back to size her up.

"I've waited a long time to thank you for loving me." He sighed. "And this time, I'm not thanking you in my head in some fantasy. It's for real."

"And just what kind of fantasies are you having about me that require such admissions, young man?"

"Well... uh... the kind that you'll have to marry me to be in, actually!" Even Silvan blushed at his comment.

"Now, Silvan! Is that a proposal?"

"Not yet. I just now got your admission of love, for cryin' out loud, woman! I gotta work up enough courage to ask for your hand, next!"

They laughed and held each other and walked on even lighter feet to the mansion in the mountain. Ariana was so ecstatic in her realized love for Silvan that she lost the chance to tell Gwendolyn about her vision. Ariana forget the scenes in her head until long after Silvan departed, leaving her with fluttering kisses all over her pale face. He smiled impishly as he always did, but with an underlying tenderness now that he had his answer. He jested and picked more deliberately. He had lain a claim to her heart long ago, before Ariana returned to the mountains. Now he had permission from the one he so cherished, and he took every opportunity to make her blush. Therefore, as Ariana— glowing with newfound love—made her way into her room that night, she overlooked a simple promise she'd made to Gwendolyn. She didn't tell her aunt of her vision.

Well into the night, weary from tossing and turning in throes of insomnia, Ariana awoke fully at the sound of her name whispered in the darkness. She listened hard and looked around her room. *No one's here!* The bright moon illuminated her white bedroom. All the furniture remained, exactly in its original spot, since she came to that room four years ago. The vanity mirror still reflected moonlight into her eyes; all her brushes and hygiene implements lined up perfectly on the dresser. The vanity table sat mostly unused, merely getting a dusting once in a while. On the top set the carved white jewelry box her mother had kept since Ariana could remember. Even now, Ariana hadn't made herself open the latch and touch the things her mother kept inside. Her mother's love for that box and its contents was surpassed only by the love of her family.

On this night, Ariana felt more drawn to it than ever, like the box spoke to her. She allowed the warm voice to draw her out of bed. She moved in her flowing gown to the table and pulled out the twisting metal chair. As she sat, her hands touched either side of the heavy box.

Apprehension took her unawares. What could be so bad about opening something left her by her mother? Ariana realized, for the first time, that she'd never seen inside the box. Her mother had made it off limits to curious little girls. *Has the time come to see what I had, of necessity, been kept from seeing?* Ariana swallowed hard, gulping past the fluttering in her throat. Her hand lifted the latch and she pulled up the heavy lid. It tilted back to show a small heart-shaped mirror on the inside, framed before a satiny lining of the deepest azure. She braved a glance into the bottom compartments of the box. Everything beneath was covered by a rectangle of paper, a thick envelope with Ariana's name written on the outside. It was her mother's beautiful handwriting.

With delicacy, she picked up the envelope and pulled out the handmade card—antique white and raised pearl accents. The words were written in a special calligraphy her mother had used, which Ariana now recognized as the elaborate style of Alcourne scribes. Her thin hands shook as she read the words. Tears sprang to her eyes.

"My dearest and only child,
My angel from heaven sent,
Through hardship you have triumphed
For your heart our lives were meant."

Ariana pressed her lips together to keep her sobbing at bay, then opened the first cover of the card. She read:

"Ariana, reading here means we have fulfilled our purpose in providing life to you. We knew all along that someday you would be in danger and sought to protect you from that. Reading this means you have gained the courage to open the box I kept from you all your life. Reading this card means that my sister Gwendolyn has found you and taught you your true past. You've probably met an incorrigible green-eyed boy who was only three when you were born, if his promise still held up."

Ariana smiled in spite of her tears.

"By now, you know your heart and body and soul. By now, you are ready for the future that binds you to the stars. I wish we could have done more, my dear. I wish we could be there in body as well as spirit. I wish we could see you, as you must be now, a strong-hearted Alcourne, loving your heritage: A woman with an honorable purpose. A creature of purity and light. Our daughter, it is time for you to shine!"

Beneath the words "Love Always," her mother's scripted signature and her father's masculine scrawl adorned the last page. Ariana sat hugging the card to her chest, a child again amid overwhelming emotion. When her eyes cleared of tears, she saw for the first time the contents of the box. Delicately laid out in every crevice were dainty pieces of jewelry and pendants. Holding her card in one hand, she reached for the pieces. Among the pieces were very naturally shaped stones and metals of all colors and types. Her hand found a single white spiral about three inches long, attached at its blunt base with a piece of silver to a heavy chain. She examined the ivory-colored coil.

"Alicorn," she whispered.

"Yes, you were still a baby when that came from your soft forehead." Gwendolyn had arrived silently at her half-closed door. "You healed so thoroughly it didn't leave a scar back then. It is the true alicorn, a baby's first. But it is one of the signs that you were to have the Great Purpose."

The small piece of alicorn slipped between her fingers. She thought she heard a baby's laughter tinkling through her head. She had a strong memory of her parents' faces as they looked down on her. "True alicorn." She gasped. "I think the box was calling to me. Is that possible?"

"Perhaps, like a message begging to be read. Your dear mother left clues to your path in her box. She experienced flashes of vision, not detailed ones like you have." Gwendolyn lifted the alicorn from Ariana's hand, smiling tenderly. "Each time, she and your father would make a piece based on what she saw… It is saturated in their essence."

In awe, Ariana shook her head. "My mother had visions, too?"

"They consumed her." Gwendolyn replaced the alicorn necklace in its center slot. "The visions were so strong she had to channel their full potency into an object, or risk her health by holding onto their power."

Ariana puzzled on the immensity of such visions. "I had a vision in the woods last evening." Ariana remembered every detail from her vision, turning from the box. "A dragon and a serpent enslaved masses of creatures who were simply…waiting…for something."

"Or someone, dear child."

Ariana's eyes widened for a moment. She gestured for Gwendolyn to sit. With hardly a whisper of air, her aunt sat down, watching from the bed. There were earrings in the shape of scaled creatures coiling around themselves. To the left was a silver barrette with a mountain scene carved into it, the trees enameled in the colors of spring. A vague outline of the mansion in the mountain was in the background. Closer, hand-in-hand, were two forms, one male and one female. The male had eyes made of tiny emeralds.

"Silvan!" Ariana gasped. "She knew about us before I did!"

Ariana beamed at Gwendolyn, who smiled and nodded. Ariana lifted an intricate orange and yellow ring from its slot. It was in the shape of a bird on fire, its wings thrown up and outward and its tail swirling toward the knuckle as its claws grabbed around the finger it now adorned.

"So much detail! It's a firebird, I suppose." Ariana turned her hand to and fro. "Am I to guess the meaning?"

"Not quite." Gwendolyn clenched her jaw. "Give it a moment."

Heat arose in the coolness. Then Ariana's room blurred from white to blazing orange and yellow and red. Blue and purple mingled with the slow burning flames, engulfing all she knew. She pinned the hand with the ring on it close to her heart. Her intricate card fell to the floor. Ariana clenched her wrist with her other hand. Her face flushed pink and sweat broke out on her scarred forehead. A voice inaudible to Gwendolyn caught Ariana's ears.

"Come soon, Unicorn. The light fades but the fire burns hotter." The voice grew weak and silent. Then the voice cried out in pain. "I can wait longer; I have waited this long. But you cannot escape that which seeks you. Soon it will devour the light you emanate. Danger comes to you, Unicorn! It is now time!"

Ariana clasped her head with both hands and fell back into her seat. The ring in the shape of a fiery bird still clung to her finger. Gwendolyn reached for her.

"What just happened, child? Tell me." Gwendolyn grasped Ariana's shoulders to steady her.

"Taiyo. Her name was Taiyo!" shrieked Ariana. "It felt like she was somewhere that was on fire! It was all she could do to even speak to me!"

Sweat poured from her forehead and dripped off her chin. Her face still felt hot like she was within the flames. She held up her burnt fingers for Gwendolyn to see. Gwendolyn pressed her lips against Ariana's fingers, helping their quick healing. Then she hugged her tightly, whispering comforting words. Bare feet skidded to a stop outside Ariana's door. Then the sleep-tousled form of Silvan spilled into the doorway and fell before his love, his green eyes filled with worry and concern.

"She said danger comes this way, and that it's time!"

Silvan was confused. "Who said that?"

"Taiyo." Then she turned to Gwendolyn. "Does she mean it's time for me to leave already? I'm scared, Aunt Gwen. This brush with... whoever she is...scares me!"

They spent the rest of the night soothing her. They pulled the ring from her finger as she finally rested. Gwendolyn replaced the lid on the jewelry box. She turned to face the young girl who slept with a slight frown contorting her smooth face. Silvan had fallen asleep. His hand held hers tightly, but his body rested awkwardly on the floor at her bedside. His head tilted upward, resting against the mattress and facing his love. Gwendolyn smiled, but her eyes were weary, her mind troubled. The visions had accelerated. Ariana saw more than mere symbols in her head. The things she saw could very well be literal creatures. Gwendolyn had prepared the girl in every way she could. She pained her heart yet again with knowledge of the hurt Ariana would need to endure. The poor child!

A thin hand caressed her throbbing temple as she gave in to a moment of weakness at the momentous events that would come. As she left the room and its exhausted occupants to the sunlit white glow of morning, Gwendolyn knew rest would prove difficult for herself as well.

*   *   *

Ariana's first feeling was the tight pressure of sweet reassurance on her hand. She squinted into the bright white light of day, reflected at all angles by her white furniture and walls. All was aglow with the vibrancy of pure sunshine. Attached to her hand was Silvan's, as he lie curled up on the floor with his head resting against her mattress. With her slight movement, he stirred. His sleepy green eyes regarded her with concern. He hauled his aching body to sit on the edge of her bed, never releasing her hand.

"Are you okay, now?" When she nodded, he glanced away. "I'm worried for you... your vision was really powerful. I think it hurt you. And I was helpless."

"You are not! I'm...fine, Silvan. Just shaken. Feels kind of like the fairy tale euphoria is wearing off." She chuckled, but it hurt her head. "I'm not sure I like that."

"I'm with you, come what may. You know that, Ariana." He kissed her hand and smiled past his worry. "You can't get rid of me all that easily, especially now that I know ya like me!"

His gorgeous smile made her grin back at him. She kissed him gently on the forehead in appreciation of his good humor. Her temples and shoulders ached with dull tension. Her mind swam with her visions. A desire to know this *Taiyo* person began to press to the forefront. With her desire came a fear that she would find out all too soon.

Spurred on by Taiyo's warning, Ariana dropped her feet to the floor and walked the short distance to her vanity table. There on the white surface was the ivory jewelry box. Silvan followed her with renewed worry.

"What do you plan to do, Ariana?" Silvan wrung his hands with worry. "If those pieces give you such intense visions, the effects may hurt you for real next time!"

"My mother meant them as teaching tools. Now I know what to expect from them. Would you please find Gwendolyn? I may need you both this time." Ariana pressed her fingers to her forehead.

"I will, but we will stop you if it gets too bad. You can't fulfill your purpose with a severed mind!" Silvan darted down the hall.

Ariana's fingertips brushed the smooth edges of the jewelry box lid. She lifted the lid and tilted it back, again looking upon the treasures her mother prepared for her. The hair barrette caught her eye again. What could only be Silvan's emerald eyes gazed up in tiny detail at Ariana, seated upon a branch and reaching down with her hand in his. She had a thin tail with long flowing hair from it and a spiral horn on her forehead. Ariana hadn't noticed those details before. She reached for the barrette cautiously. When it was in her hands she felt a tingle in her mind, and a physical tremor leapt up her arms through her hands. No pain followed it this time. Only a fluttering vibrated her heart and muscles and organs. Ariana was compelled to stand, letting the comforting feeling caress her. A voice echoed hollowly in her mind. It was a familiar one:

"It is time, Unicorn!"

"Taiyo!" she said, recognizing the source. "I have questions!"

The voice left as it had come. Abruptly. Ariana frowned in annoyance at the cryptic way this Taiyo handled herself. Then the tingling shifted to her spine. A jolting shaft of pain descended her spinal column. Her teeth clenched as she bit back a scream. On the barrette she saw through teary eyes that part of it was glowing faintly white. The tail of the silver-carved Ariana was vaguely luminous. Ariana gasped as heat gathered in her back. The base of her spine split from her back. From each segment of bone formed another and another, creating a longer appendage with each heartbeat. Musculature and skin followed the curving path of alicorn-laden bone. A fine, downy hair covered the new tail, and long, silky hair began to grow in waves a third of the way up from the tip.

Her bare wrists and ankles sprouted the same fine white hair that appeared at the end of her new tail. As she watched in wordless amazement, the hair grew longer and wavy, like the feathering at the ankles of her favorite Friesian horses. Her finger and toenails took on a deeper blue-purple tinge, hardening into blue-horn consistency found in horse-hoof. The pain died away as soon as her tail stopped growing. Ariana pulled up the hem of her gown and saw the slender graceful tail droop to her ankles. She furrowed her brow and concentrated. The tail moved a bit. She flexed the new muscles and began to control it.

"I have a freaking unicorn tail!" She stuck her tongue out and concentrated harder. It moved again.

Thus did Gwendolyn and Silvan find her, with the hem of her gown raised to knee level as she twitched her new tail, with oddly long hair at her wrists and ankles and a pensive expression on her tear-streaked face.

Silvan panicked, darted into the room and skidded to a stop when he saw nothing he could do. Gwendolyn watched in silence, unsurprised by the new addition to Ariana's body. Ariana found the whole situation quite unusual, even for something that happened to her.

"I held the barrette, Aunt Gwen." She squinted in concentration. The tail twitched. "That's all. Then my body tingled and hurt and decided I needed a tail, I think. And Taiyo told me that it's time again."

Her matter-of-fact tone caused Gwendolyn's lips to curve in a smile. Gwendolyn looked at the barrette still clasped in Ariana's hand. Then she sat on the edge of the white bed. "So even a mere brush with those who know your purpose can trigger a transformation? Such power, from so obvious a distance. This Taiyo is who leads you, through your mother's creations."

"You're not surprised, not even a little, that Ariana has sprouted a tail and various other additions?" Silvan gestured wildly and with great concern. "I knew she had a big purpose, but you never said anything about this! A literal, physical transformation?"

"She has taken a step closer to the original power of our ancestors by regaining aspects of their physical appearance. No doubt we will discover that her powers are now heightened. It seems perfectly natural to me, Silvan." Gwendolyn blinked at the boy, her face a mask of logic.

"You don't like it, Silvan?" Ariana cast him a sheepish grin. She still looked down at the tail with new surprise each time she moved it.

"I never said that. I can see several... advantages to such a thing, later on." His old grin was back as he teased a blushing Ariana in front of her aunt. "But...both of you are very nonchalant about something this new! That's what confuses me!"

"The fact that this signifies a new step forward in her purpose has nothing to do with your chagrin, Silvan?" Gwendolyn folded her hands in her lap.

"No. Well, maybe. A little." He lowered his green eyes.

"Silvan?"

"Yes, my Ariana?" Silvan raised his flushed face to hers.

"I've got a new tail. I'm surprised you haven't asked to touch it." She teased with a blushing smile. She saw Gwendolyn roll her eyes.

"I'm surprised you think I would ask such a thing, young lady! I'm definitely not the sort for such things, I'll have you know!" He stepped back in exasperated shock as he wagged a thin finger at her.

"Oh, goodness!" Gwendolyn sighed in equally mock disgust, throwing her hands into the air. "I suppose I may leave if you've had quite enough excitement for one day, Ariana?"

"Yeah, Aunt Gwen." She dug through her dresser. "Sorry, but I think I should spend some time with it to see if it's as much aggravation as Silvan."

"Hey!" Silvan pouted as Gwendolyn rose to leave, laughing at his expense.

"I expect a full report by sundown on your findings." Gwendolyn left.

Ariana turned to close the jewelry box. She paused with the silver barrette in hand. She smiled and gathered her long hair, clasping the barrette firmly toward the back of her head. *Such a pretty thing should be worn, if it has served its purpose.*

When she turned back to Silvan, he sat on her bed. His expression was full of adoration and mischief, a combination Ariana found delightful in him. She reached for his outstretched hand and squeezed it.

"So, can I?" Silvan's face was a mask of innocence.

"Can you what?"

"Touch your new tail, of course!"

"You scoundrel!" Ariana shoved his shoulder. "As a matter of fact, I don't think you qualify yet."

"When will that be, then?"

"Oh, I'll let you know!" Then she turned and sat next to him, her tail curling around and forward to allow her to sit.

Ariana leaned forward and pressed her lips to his in a thankful kiss, before he could say another word. His silver hair fell forward and touched her face. His green eyes closed, his brow drawn together in unexpressed worry. He kissed her a bit hard, trying to keep a desperate hold on her any way he could, while he was still allowed.

Ariana felt his arms pull her hard against his chest. She melted in his passionately desperate kiss, loving him as much for his love as his concern, for she had felt the winds of change bringing something disastrous upon her even now. Her new form might bring new power, but still she suffered with her burden, a burden along a path no one else could walk.

*   *   *

The pair jumped straight into sprints and hand to hand battle. Ariana discovered a great boost in her strength, speed, healing and recovery time. This comforted Silvan throughout the day, but made him cautious. She would be more powerful, after all. *There's no way I can dodge her now*. He finally breathed a sigh of relief when she elbowed him in the face. The tenderness of his cheek was proof that she had finally surpassed her teacher. And the way she apologized was proof that she regretted it. He drank in the attention, and got right back to work.

Gwendolyn chased after them with prepared meals because, in their excitement, they'd forgotten to eat. Evening fell and all were in good spirits. Night arrived and all were exhausted. Silvan walked Ariana to her room and lingered at the door. She invited him inside for a bit, but he tore himself away and trudged down the hallway.

Alone in his room, Silvan imagined a time without worry. He wanted to experience it once more. Before, he had no reason to worry—no one to worry about. Now was different. He lost sleep to long hours of concern. He tried to come to conclusions, to make plans and decisions. Ariana filled him with so much love and caring, yet she was bound to leave sooner rather than later. She grew distant in her own worries.

Silvan sighed heavily and sank back into his bed. Messy gray hair filtered the moonlight from his emerald eyes. His well-defined bare chest rose and fell in a steady rhythm, but his mind raced. All his life he'd longed for the one he promised to protect. She came, and he protected and taught her. He loved her at first sight. She even loved him in return. In his mind, he replayed every shy blush and elegant movement and every sweet word her pure heart spoke. He wanted so much to keep her from her task—a task for which she didn't even know the details. In fact, he just wanted to keep her, to have her near him and safe always. He knew he couldn't make that choice.

He'd fallen in love. He'd held her in his mind so often that he wished he could hold her in reality. He'd dreamed of her soft, pale body and sweet, low voice almost every moment he slept. He was not allowed, though. She slept just down the hall from him. He imagined he could hear her soft breath and see her lovely sleeping form and pale face in the moonlight. She might even welcome him. Yet he was not allowed to go to her. He was not allowed to make real his promise of marriage. Not yet. All his heart and body desired her. But he knew, as everyone else knew, that to face the evil that presented itself in her future, she must be pure in every way: mind, heart, soul, and body. Lacking purity and innocence, she would fail.

His ongoing personal torment reminded him of this. Yet every time he hugged her or kissed her, he felt his love swelling inside of him. He'd waited so long to have her as his wife, and now he must wait, and keep her secure: for protection was part of his job. So he hid his true love in his teasing. He fought for reserve when touching her. He tore away his mouth from her hungry, searching lips when he most wanted to let her know the truth of his feelings. He had to keep control.

A soft knock sounded at his door. His heart skipped as he was torn from his worries. He unwound the blankets from his legs and walked across the small room. He could hear his heartbeat as he looked upon Ariana standing at his door in her sheer nightgown. She carried a small tray with a teapot and two cups, his vision of a perfect hostess.

"I was having trouble sleeping. It's chamomile. Will you join me?"

Silvan ran his hand through his sweaty hair. Sweat gleamed on his bare chest. "Please." He pulled the door open for her. "Looks like you toss and turn and look much better afterward than I."

"You think I don't sweat, then?"

"Girls don't sweat. It's proven. They 'glow'."

"Ah, I see." Ariana set down the tray on his nightstand. "Well, shame on whoever spread that rumor!"

Silvan reached for his shirt.

"No need. Midnight tea doesn't require a collar, Silvan." She gave him an appreciative glance, making his heart pound and face redden.

Ariana poured steaming tea, dropping sugars and pouring warm milk in the chamomile for both. She stirred and turned to Silvan. She sat on the edge of his bed and patted the place beside her. She placed the dish and cup in his hand and reached for her own. They drank the soothing tea in silence, letting the steam caress their worries away. He finished his drink first, settled the cup on the saucer with a clink, and watched her small smile. Her eyes were closed. He got a rare chance to just stare at her peaceful face. Her eyes opened before he could look away. She set her cup on the tray and reached for his. Their hands brushed briefly in the action.

Ariana leaned toward him and stared into his emerald eyes. He felt his heart jump as always. She leaned forward and kissed him. Silvan startled with the sudden movement then reveled in the feel of her soft lips against his. Silvan almost succumbed to his deeper concern for his beloved. The events of the past couple days loomed to block out his hope of deterring her departure. And yet she kissed him. He clenched his hands so as not to touch her. He was scared. Her sweet mouth and shadowy violet eyes entranced him, so he closed his eyes.

She pulled him toward her as she leaned back onto the bed. His heart pounded harder. For the very first time, he kissed her with all the passion and love and worry he sought to suppress. He almost crushed her to him, an embrace far harsher than he intended. But she gasped a little and clung to him with the same passion he gave her. She kissed him just as hungrily.

Finally, he pulled away, gasping for air, his mouth trembling. Ariana leaned on an elbow, gazing at him with a small mysterious smile. Her eyes beckoned him. Her hand fell to clutch his, sending fire through his veins. She was catching her breath, too. But her chest rose and fell in a more enticing rhythm to Silvan's wandering gaze. They had both grown up in the four years they were together, in every way possible. Silvan snapped his eyes to hers, smiling in worry.

"Never doubt that I love you, my Ariana," he said between shaky breaths.

"I never intend to doubt you." She slid nearer and put her arms around his neck.

"I might not be able to stop myself from..." he stammered.

"I'll end the night with my innocence intact. Don't worry."

With that, she pulled his face toward her and he leaned forward into a sweeter kiss than he'd ever shared with her. A long kiss, followed by another and another. Her hands slid over his back. His arm was around her with the other hand cupping her pale face. For long hours they held each other.

Though desire flared between them, Ariana kept her promise of innocence. When his hands wandered, she caught them in hers. When his mouth wandered, she brought it back to hers. When her hands wandered, she clenched them against his back. When her mouth wandered, she bit her lips together. Many times she reached for the waistband of his pants only to pull her hands away as Silvan stifled a low moan.

She kissed him once more and pulled away to smile at his wild hair and bare chest. He saw her mouth trembling in a shy smile and in desire. He knew she was going to leave before she lost control. She stood and backed toward the table, whispering loving words and good nights. He leapt to his feet. He put his arms around her, feeling the full press of her body yet again. She giggled at his touch. She was trembling all over.

"Did I go too far? I'm so sorry!"

"No, my dear Silvan. I promised, remember?" she whispered with a smile.

With that, she turned and walked out of the room, pulling her body from his embrace. He strode to the door and watched the longest walk he'd ever seen her take. He never had a heart so full of the sweetness that only she could impart to him. Even in the predawn hours, Silvan was still catching his breath. His body trembled in every place she had touched him: along his back and sides and chest. Along his hips, too. A tremor ran through his body as he remembered Ariana reaching for his waistband. So close, and yet going any further would have shattered them both. He squirmed in bed. Yet again, he couldn't sleep. Instead of exhausted, he was energized. She knew just how much he loved her. Not the full extent, but as much as he could show her with kisses and words.

Then came the guilty worry. Creeping between the peaks of elation in his mind were threads of concern. Everything occurred for a reason, in its time. He knew this and to himself and Ariana he gave his silent promise, to live, and keep her alive long enough to realize their purpose together. And to love, no matter the consequence. Though his heart still thudded and his body tingled, he found the promise exhausting, draining all his energy. Then he slipped into a light sleep of mixed dreams, where Ariana spoke in her low voice into his ear and kissed him, sending tremors through his body. She pulled his pants down past his hips and sat delicately in his lap. She began to lift her gown over her head. Instead of the pale, perfect body he expected, a red scaly creature with wings replaced her and tore out her throat before she could scream, while Silvan could only bat at it with weak hands.

Silvan awoke in terror, crying out in his fear. He sat upright with his palms digging into his eyes to clear them of the grotesque picture. The creature had an evil laugh that followed him to waking. He looked around his darkened bedroom. Nothing moved. He crept to the door, looking all about him as he padded down the hallway, his bare chest ghostly in the dimness. Ariana's door was slightly ajar. He leaned into it a fraction. She slept soundly, her breast rising and falling steadily beneath the thin white gown. A hand rested carelessly beside her face on the pillow. A peaceful smile lit her face and sent warmth through Silvan's worried heart. He almost went to her, but decided against it.

Back in his warm bed, he pulled the blankets up around his chin, like he was a child again. A chill settled over the mountain and seemingly into his room. Silvan curled up fetal-style and hugged his knees. He couldn't save her in his dream, but it was only a dream, right? The scene replayed itself in his mind, so jarring that tears slipped from his eyes onto his pillow. He cried like a kid, biting his lips to keep mournful wails from escaping. His shoulders shuddered. His breath tore out in ragged gasps. The coldness would not go away. The sight of his beloved torn apart by the red-scaled creature never left his mind. Well into daylight, he cried, finding no comfort from within.

Only the brightness of the sunlight broke him from despair. It reminded him of his love's smile as she wrapped her arms around him. He pulled himself into a sitting position and lowered his feet to the floor. His head pounded from his tears. He squinted beneath heavy eyelids. His body protested with a half dozen pops and cracks when he stood and walked toward his closet to get dressed.

"Way to prove I need to knock first!"

His jaw dropped before his shorts dropped, luckily. Ariana stood there, openly admiring his lean, cut body. Still she blushed. This time, Silvan blushed too. She wore a sleek blue half-sleeve, half-leg suit she used for training. Her long tail swept behind her, twitching side to side ever so slightly. The feathering at her wrists and ankles, for that was what they determined it was, fell in short waves to mirror her long, wavy white hair, pulled back in her barrette with long strands falling forward. She was gorgeous.

Bedsore and swollen faced from his hard night, Silvan smiled at her with his puffy eyes. She smiled back and said that he looked like he hadn't slept. He admitted he hadn't. His silky long hair stood at odd angles from his head. His shoulders slumped slightly. Still she smiled at him.

"I look like crap, and you're smiling at me?"

"You're beautiful." Ariana grinned. "I like looking at lovely creatures."

Though she blushed profusely, he tingled at her comment. Ariana made comical attempts to tuck his hair behind his ears, then kissed his mouth lightly.

"Besides, if I'm to be with you so long, I guess I have to see you in every... incarnation. I've seen the teasing Silvan, and the loving Silvan, and this seems to be the I'm-still-cute-though-I-haven't-slept-a-bit Silvan. I like them all."

"Like?"

"Well, 'love,' I suppose."

"You suppose!" He feigned shock.

"I know," she purred and kissed him on the cheek.

"On the cheek." He pouted.

"Don't push your luck, Silvan."

Then she was out, blushingly playful as always. He took heart from her enthusiasm and dressed quickly to join her for their meal. He forgot his dream for the day. *Probably just a figment of my worried imagination.* At least, he hoped.

7: THE BLOOD RUBY

In the forest graveyard, a dark-cloaked figure loomed. Towering above the stones, the form stooped and moved among the stones, speaking the names thereon with disgust in a throaty dialect foreign to the race of Alcournes currently living in the surrounding mountains. Those of the more ancient race, buried in older graves, would have recognized it instantly. They would have warned the human-form creatures to flee. But they could not speak. They were no longer among their bones. They could not warn of the dark creature of legend that walked among them. They could not protect their heirs from its deception, nor of the certain destruction they all faced. All who slept in the graveyard knew the creature.

The tall figure stopped at two graves dug only in recent years. The names here did not interest the ethereal creature. A long arm reached out. A large, long-fingered hand wreathed in silver rings spread over the flower-strewn resting place of the woman. The flowers there died and shrank away. The dirt was bare beneath the shriveled vegetation. The creature knelt there a moment, staring at the tombstone, then plunged a silver-ringed hand into the dirt. A gauntleted forearm followed, until the entire arm probed the grave. A slight hiss of accomplishment followed. The arm reemerged, the hand clenched around a pale object.

Another silver-strewn hand pulled away a rotted cloth cover—a glove. Finger bones gleamed unnaturally white in the moonlight amid remnants of rotted flesh. A glinting ring encircled the forefinger bone. The silver-ringed figure reached for it. As living fingers pulled the ruby stone from its place, the live fingers sizzled. Smoke curled up where the silvered fingers slid over bone. The thin sheath of alicorn still fought against the dark evil that handled it. The figure laughed and placed the blood-red stone on its own long finger, amid the other silver rings. The creature cast the corpse's hand across the graveyard with a flick of its wrist, shattering the bones against a larger tombstone.

"My pet will be well pleased," spoke two voices, baritone and soprano, from the darkness of the hood.

The silver-ringed hands with a heavy ruby among them reached for the edges of the hood. They pulled back the dark cloth to reveal the face of an angel, pale and smooth. The mouth was oddly shaped, with a prominent but steeply curved upper lip and a narrow lower lip. The straight nose thrust out, but with no great proportion. The wide eyes peered out, blank and staring, lined first with brightest red that smoldered in the moon's light, then darkened with sweeping charcoal shadows and heavy black lines. The iridescent ice blue irises glowed brilliantly between the redlined eyelids.

From the high forehead grew a three-pronged silver crown of horns, an extension of the face rather than an accessory. Thin, high eyebrows matched the unusually colored hair. At once the cloak-covered hair seemed to seethe with unearthly movement. It was wavy, then straight, then curled. It was pale blonde, then gray, then red, then brown all in the span of seconds. The creature with shifting hair straightened its shoulders once more. Pushing the great cloak behind her shoulders, she revealed a muscular woman's body, clad in silver armor that molded to every curve. Her large bust and much of her shoulder was tattooed on her left side with a winged red lizard that pulsed in the darkness.

"Perhaps these deceptive creatures, these unicorns, will prove worthy sport for me tonight. I'd hate to go back home without the head of their prodigy on my platter." The air rang with the woman's oddly alluring double voice.

She smiled. She stared at her muddy gauntlet, then at the ruby on her other hand. With a rustling of her cloak and a blur of movement, she leapt into the air and traversed the mountains beyond. She killed along a circular route, trying to find the hidden mansion she had learned about only recently—the mansion that hid the presence of the Purposed Unicorn from her.

She smelled the blood of unicorns and heard their pounding hearts, but none held her interest for very long. None would *tell* her very much. Her first victims died quickly. Later victims suffered longer. She would smoke out the elusive one with the torture of her brethren. Screams of hideous fatality and terror rose in the night. Confusion led to chaotic pandemonium as a reign of destruction filled the air with the scent of innocent blood. Above it all, the giantess clad in silver laughed, a horrendous cackle of bloodlust and power.

*　　　*　　　*

Fully awake at the first sound of carnage near the mansion, Ariana breathed in gasps. Around her room, ghostly snakes writhed in the aftermath of an incomplete dream. The threat at long last was upon her, only two days since her transformation. She had reached for piece after piece of her mother's prophetic jewelry with a frightening premonition that she would not have time to learn all she needed. She was right.

On her feet, she cinched on the wide belt packed with supplies. She scooped her mother's jewelry into a larger pouch and zipped it closed. She grabbed other items arranged on her dresser for this occasion and shoved them into the belt in a frantic rush. She threw on her earth-colored travel clothes. Finally, she found the other pack of nonperishable food supplies and slung it over her shoulder.

Gwendolyn made it quite obvious what the plan of escape was to be, in case of a night attack. The horde outside would be hunting all the Alcournes in search of Ariana. They had no choice but to run. Ariana's power was not yet strong enough to kill such a force. Ariana trembled every time she heard the screams of her brethren. Her fear and training moved her feet. Her determination made her ready to fight if need be. She ran out of her room, heard the cries and felt the detachment and hollow noise as in a dream. Were these her feet and hands? Was this her wildly beating heart? Her mind swam.

She skidded into Silvan, who had just made it to her door. His green eyes held more fear than she'd ever seen in them. But he was prepared, carrying more than she but moving just as lightly on his feet. Not a word spoken, he grabbed her shoulder and pulled her along to Gwendolyn's corner bedchamber. The older woman had already dressed and gathered her scant supplies. She had a look of despair at leaving so much behind. So many lives lost already!

"We were prepared." Gwendolyn trembled. "We trained and learned and tried so hard! They're so strong. How can they all die so easily?"

"Aunt Gwen, the enemy is close." Silvan grabbed her arm and dragged her toward the tunnels. "We leave now!"

Ariana watched Gwendolyn's dismayed face and knew she still hoped to return one day to this long-dead way of life, a day when good conquers evil and Atlantis could unite the world again. The others knew this would come to pass one day—the renewed destruction of their way of life. With their final screams, they served those who fled, allowing them to track the destruction. Gwendolyn, Silvan and Ariana heard sounds of torture for the identity of the Personification of the Unicorn. Where was she? All knew something of the answer. Each died with dignity, denying the enemy his or her knowledge.

Through a narrow passage beneath the mountain, the group left behind the last of their family. Gwendolyn sealed the way behind them. Ariana's feet hit the dirt running, in complete silence and darkness, having tread the path many times in training. The suffocating silence left each with their thoughts for far too long. *Too fast, too powerful, too brutal.* This enemy killed at a rate Ariana couldn't fathom. Emerging from the musty tunnel into the forest, the air rushed past, drowning out the massacre from far behind them. *Had no one followed procedure? Did they even have time?* Then Ariana's heart trembled. *Are they all dead? Every last one?*

Her steps slowed. *Are they suffering because of me?* She stopped dead in her tracks and looked back. *All dead because of me.* Her sight grew dim. The roaring of the wind in her ears ceased. The hollowness of her dream-like state snapped. Silvan shook her and hissed her name in a harsh whisper. The sound came to her from very far away. Of this she was vaguely aware.

When her eyes cleared, she focused for the first time on her surroundings. Familiar landmarks zipped past. Ariana felt her feet flying beneath her. Somehow, he must have forced her to move. She knew she was running again. Silvan released her hand when the light returned to her eyes. His determined stare sobered her, forcing her to continue. Along a steep ravine, she felt like she could run forever. The wind in her ears returned, and with each step, she regained herself, pushing away the creeping numbness with another stride.

Deep into the mountains they fled, possibly the only three among hundreds to survive. The sounds of death disappeared as they ran with their almost supernatural grace and speed to a place far from home. They found the cave that led to a narrow path along a cliff and took it at twice their normal speed, leaving hardly a dent in the dry soil. Gwendolyn kept pace like a youth, despite being the oldest of them all. She had to lead them. It was one of her final duties to the Fated Alcourne. The Purposed One.

Well into the next morning they ran. Ariana no longer recognized any mountain around her. Every tree was a vague blur as they ran. Her endurance training served her well. Only recently had she begun to tire. The others felt the effects as well. Gwendolyn was the first to slow and stop.

"We are at a half-way point to your new sanctuary, Ariana. Do you remember the path I taught you?"

"Of course!" Ariana took a few cleansing breaths. "But don't act like you won't be with us!"

"Perhaps I will." Gwendolyn had a distant look in her eyes.

"No! You will." Ariana gasped. "So much death. All of our people. By now, we're the only ones left! I can't bear that they died...that they're *dying*...because of me! It's too much!" The adrenaline from their flight drained from her.

"It's not your fault, Ariana! They love you. They prepared for this day!" Silvan tried to hold her. She shrugged him off.

"It is my fault! They're all so pure and innocent!" Ariana flung her bag to the ground in frustration and exhaustion. "Blameless! And yet they fall, dead for something they don't even know I can do!"

"Faith, Ariana. As long as you're alive, there is hope that your blood will bring forth the new Atlantis," Gwendolyn cried. "They may be pure, some may be innocent. But don't relegate their sacrifice to a single, selfish cause so you alone can shoulder the burden." She clung to Ariana's shoulders, seething in anger. "They die so the very heart of Atlantis, the soul of peace, may live on. Carry the weight of their deaths if you will. But until your corpse rots in the earth, they have not died in vain!" Gwendolyn's full authority and bearing restored, she held the sobbing, rattled girl against her chest. "Now, we must rest only briefly, before our plan is further detected by our enemies."

Ariana ate in silence, dirt smudged and weary and hurting for the loss of family and friends. Gwendolyn's words rang in her head and seared into her heart. Never before had she seen Gwendolyn so angry. *I'm just one person, just a silly girl after all.* She stared at the crust of bread in her hand, at the dark and white swirl inside the marble rye. Some dear baker had taken great care to form the swirl into a heart just for Gwendolyn's household. And that very baker would have gladly died to keep the enemy from Ariana. All of them, young and old, died with such poise and dignity. *Aunt Gwen must be suffering more than either of us!* Gwendolyn had witnessed the birth of the oldest and heard the first cries of the youngest for so many generations. *How foolish to think I am alone in my suffering!* Tears streamed down Ariana's cheeks. She felt silly for hugging the slice of bread to her heart, but took courage in the perspective she gained.

When at last she stood, Ariana felt a new energy in her body. She would run forever if needed. She would move beyond any obstacle placed in her path. She would live and fight and win at all costs. She would make her life so full that the dead could look down with pride at her resolve. And one day, when she figured out the trick of it, she would restore the wisdom of Atlantis to the whole weary world. Right after she murdered the bastards responsible for this and past bloodshed.

Catching the others' stony glances, she nodded.

"Let's go."

Then they started out once more, for a new sanctuary promised by Gwendolyn. Slower in pace than last night's sprint, they covered ground faster than any human or animal. Gwendolyn kept them beneath forest canopies and rocky outcroppings. Occasionally, she glanced skyward as she ran, as if wary of a threat from above. Ariana wondered, but was unwilling to break their heavy, tense silence.

As the sun reached its peak and began its slow descent toward the horizon, they climbed a tree-heavy slope with large rocks jutting from between the gnarled trunks. Ahead appeared a sandy clearing bleached white with the sun's glare. A large shadow passed overhead from behind them and blocked the brilliance. A faint rushing of air broke the silence around the trio. Gwendolyn gasped and ordered them to seek cover.

From her dark perch in a high branch of the coarse tree, Ariana saw the new arrival. A dark-cloaked giant, slender and menacing, stepped with dignity and purpose into the clearing. When it reached the opening between the trees, it paused and whirled to face the gathering darkness therein. The only light that allowed Ariana to see the creature's face glowed from its silvery blue eyes that peered coldly into the forest.

"I continue to track you." A resonating double-voice rang out. "I kill your kin, all of them. I destroy your homes. I seek you out, but you elude me." The creature's voice raised several octaves into a clear, trilling female range. "But only until now."

The giant figure slipped into the shadowy stand of trees and rocks. The smell of blood and death preceded her. She pulled back her heavy hood, revealing moon-bright eyes along with a marble-white face and silver crown trailed by hair that shifted in color and composition with the slightest movement.

"Now I find you and require your lives for the inconvenience. None can remain alive." She laughed.

"Even the dead are not safe."

In the dim light, she raised her right hand, palm facing her. Amid silver bands stacked on the slender fingers set a large ruby. Ariana gasped. Her mother's ring! The only jewelry she took to the grave with her! She gritted her teeth at the blatant desecration, but a new thought stilled her. What if the ring had been imbued with special qualities, like the other jewelry? Was there another reason this monster acquired it?

"It is of the Blood of the Fated One, the one from whom I take this." The giantess answered Ariana's silent question. "And that blood is inside one who is close, even now. Not nearly enough blood, though, for my needs. Just enough to guide me to the one I fail to destroy. Yet, I sense fear in the heart of the Unicorn!"

Ariana folded her hand to her chest and, with a small prayer that she wouldn't miss, shoved the alicorn down the length of her fingers. *She already knows I'm here. There is no escape, is there?* She projected the alicorn darts at the alien creature. The slender silver-ringed hand passed in front of her face, deflecting three of the alicorn darts. The remaining two glanced off a silver gauntlet that emerged from the thick cloak beneath the raised hand. Into the ground and bark the alicorn burrowed, ineffective and useless. Ariana willed her throbbing hand to heal quickly, and it did.

The huge woman leaned her head back and closed her eyes, breathing deeply. "It hurts you, Fated Unicorn. And it fails. Show yourself."

"Hurt?" Ariana felt her blood boil in fury. "What do you know about pain? About fate?" Ariana was on the ground the next second, fury and fear steeling her for death.

"What do I know? I know how to cause hurt." The wide mouth parted in a smile. She ran her long fingers over her breasts and down her sides, streaking through the blood that drenched her. "I stink of that particular skill. And it is a glorious aroma!"

"You monster!" Ariana stepped from behind the tree, her fists balled and her eyes red with anger. "You kill my only living family, and have the gall to make jokes? Who are you? Give yourself a name!"

"I am many names and lives. I am physical and not. I am a lie and the truth. I am a savior and a devil."

"Enough!" Ariana pointed an indignant finger at her. "Are you Taiyo?"

Laughter rolled forth from the creature, lilting and indulgent. "Dear child, my next and most delicious victim, this Taiyo you speak of is quite opposite of me. She is without merit toward higher aims. She is useless. I am power!"

Ariana faltered. *Then Taiyo is no enemy or, even worse, no one who could answer my questions? Then who could she be? Where does she fit in if not to impact my purpose?* Everything Ariana thought she had learned about Taiyo fell apart before her.

The she-monster answered her thoughts. "Taiyo burns in a fire of her choosing, Unicorn. Darkness is all around. She burns, unable to die, because Time is bound and Night is tethered. No one can free them."

The taunting jolted Ariana, who stood still in confusion. *What is truth?* Why did the words of the monster keep her mind cloudy? She tried to remember the fire, the heat she felt when Taiyo spoke to her. *No one can free them.*

"As for my name: in this form, that of a pale woman, I am called Chandra, for my eyes glow like the moon. Otherwise, you will not know me." Chandra shifted her weight to one side. "But I tire of your curiosity, Unicorn. Now is the time of your death."

Chandra reached with a long hand and unfastened the heavy, blood-soaked cloak. She threw it in a heap across a rock. The cloth slapped wetly upon the tan stone, red blood draining from it in bright runnels upon the light surface. Chandra's body was pale, but not naturally so. With her waist long hair constantly shifting behind her crown and her pale skin occasionally blurring with some unknown effort, the only constant was the soft sheen of her skin-bonded silver armor and the steady cold stare of ice-blue eyes. A long leathery cape clung about her shoulders, light in color like the shimmer of her skin and stained with the blood of a thousand slain Alcournes. The cape fastened on two sets of claw-shaped hooks above her breast. Chandra stroked one of her cape hooks thoughtfully as the blood ruby glistened on her finger. She glared down at the small figure of Ariana with a one-sided smirk, as if in pleasure of blood to come.

In the brief seconds that followed, in a tense and fearful stare-down, Ariana gathered the alicorn in her arms. Her blood dripped on the sandy earth as she pushed a heavy spike out of each elbow and long spears from her wrists. Still she looked steadily into the chilling eyes of the monster, Chandra. She gripped the bases of the forearm spears as they reached the length of short swords.

"I see you wish to make a struggle out of your final moments. So be it."

"I wish to bring death in these final moments, Chandra!" Ariana spat at her.

She flipped her wrists upward, snapping off the spears at their base while gritting her teeth against the sobering pain. Ariana took her battle stance. *Is this the battle I have been training for? Is this the purpose of my existence?*

"Then let us bring death together!" Gwendolyn stepped out into the light, a vision of determination and strength.

Silvan landed squarely on Ariana's right, his double short swords drawn and ready for battle. His beautiful face was grim. "You forgot my promise, Ariana. I'll be the one to protect you, now and always!"

Surrounded by those remaining in her race, she felt grimly comforted.

"The Matriarch arrives. It has been such a long time," crooned Chandra.

"Earth too difficult to conquer last time, Monster?" Gwendolyn asked in an acid tone that Ariana had never witnessed. "Seems you met with a bit of resistance back then?"

"Patience, dear Matriarch! Time is fleeting. Your life has been longer than most, but will expire long before you witness my Empire!"

"We stopped you once!" She held her palm out to the creature. "I held your heart in my hand!"

"Merely delayed the inevitable, Unicorn."

"Hah! Your power isn't eternal!"

"I've heard you say that before, yet here I am, Matriarch. Did you think you'd drained me so completely that I could not return? The drain merely preserved your life, it seems." Chandra grinned down at the trio. "How does it feel living on stolen power?"

Ariana watched the exchange, her confusion mounting. *I held your heart in my hand...* echoed again and again in her head. She glanced at Silvan, who stared ahead, his face a blank mask. Silvan nodded to Ariana. He turned back to keep Chandra in his sight.

"Gwendolyn sealed the creature?!" Ariana gasped.

"Yes," came the steady voice of Gwendolyn. "And I have willed myself to live long enough to see that it's done again!"

"But you were in human form by that time!"

"Just like you are now, Ariana." Gwendolyn grinned viciously. "And no less an Alcourne!"

"You're right!" Ariana screamed and darted toward the enemy.

She lunged forward into the giant creature's path, her alicorn spears seeking a hold in the white and silver blur that was Chandra. A metallic clang stopped her thrust each time as silver gauntlets intercepted her attacks. Chandra merely slipped aside when Ariana lunged at her, gazing down with amusement through icy glowing eyes. Her crooked smile proved her good humor at the Unicorn's fruitless attempts. Ariana began to despair, never getting so much as a nick on the woman.

Ariana leapt skyward with a mighty effort and grabbed at a high branch of a gnarled tree with one arm, her spears still gripped in either hand. She pulled herself up several feet above Chandra's head and dangled unsteadily there. Of course, the giantess followed her quick movement and turned to grab Ariana's ankles.

As Ariana hoped, Silvan dove with his swords at Chandra, diverting her for a moment. Silvan danced out of her grasp. He dove forward, danced back, and tried to keep his distance.

Ariana clambered to her feet on the sturdy branch. She gritted her teeth as Chandra's fist landed a punch in Silvan's chest. She saw him sail through the air and land near Gwendolyn. Ariana also saw her only opening for attack. Chandra's back was to her. In her high perch, Ariana crossed her forearms, spears facing forward in clenched fists. Then she jumped. The quick rush of air pulled up her long white hair and ripped at her clothes. Then she felt the alicorn bury deep into Chandra's back, through the leathery silver-gray cape and into something thicker. Ariana landed in a hard crouch, dragging the spears down with her momentum.

The reaction was immediate. An inhuman shriek pierced the empty air and echoed through the sandy forest. Wisps of smoke swirled from the wounds Ariana had made. Long white arms grabbed at her back. Dark blood spiraled around the alicorn and toward the hands that still held them. Ariana stared, astonished, when the cape bled as well. It was part of Chandra.

The next things Ariana saw were furious glowing eyes staring over a broad shoulder. Before she could move aside, Chandra's gauntleted arm swung around, elbowing Ariana in the face. Several feet away, the base of an old tree jarred her still.

*   *   *

"Ariana!" screamed Silvan as he gripped his bruised chest.

He made a move to attack Chandra. Gwendolyn grabbed his arm to stop him. Instead, the Matriarch Alcourne herself leapt between Ariana and Chandra, dragging Silvan behind her. She withdrew a slender sword from her cloak and braced herself with the sword held firmly in both hands.

"I destroy her now, whether you protect her or not, Old One."

"What keeps you from it, Beast?" snarled Gwendolyn. "A sudden weakness?"

"Beast? Hmmm." Chandra's eyes flashed. "This minor wound is nothing."

"But it burns you." Gwendolyn beamed with a triumphant smile. "You feel the pain! She will purify the evil you have brought upon us, and fulfill a purpose you have failed in suppressing. More than once have you failed, Monster, if my guess is right."

"One tests the waters to see if they hold the proper amount of poison, Old Woman! Circumstance once kept me from her, but no more!" Chandra stared at Silvan, who tried in vain to wake Ariana. The creature scoffed. "The Unicorn you protect hasn't the fire to drive me back!"

Gwendolyn narrowed her eyes. "Then I, a being who *has* driven you back, will help her gain that fire!"

True, she thought. *Not yet.* Ariana lay unconscious behind her. Silvan tended to her, keeping a wary eye on Chandra and one hand on the hilt of a sword. Ariana wasn't ready yet. Soon, though, she would have the fire to destroy this monster by herself! Gwendolyn believed it with all her heart. Ariana would destroy Chandra and avenge her brethren, and restore Atlantean peace to the world. And somewhere along the line, she would encounter a greater purpose, a grander destiny. She had to make it out of this place alive, first. Gwendolyn gritted her teeth against the inevitable.

"Silvan, take her! You know where to go. Protect her at all costs, even that of your life!" Gwendolyn's voice shook with such passion that Silvan stared wide-eyed at her, fully grasping her intentions. "She will live to avenge us. See to that!"

"Aunt Gwen... no."

"No, Silvan! Go now! Remember your vow!"

Silvan's face sobered under his furrowed brow. Lips clamped shut, he lifted Ariana, dropping her across his shoulder before turning once more to Gwendolyn. His eyes said, "I love you" to the woman who raised him.

"I know..." she whispered with her back to him. "I love you both. That's why..."

Silvan nodded and darted between the trees. He never learned stealth as well as Ariana, but well enough to escape Chandra's searching eyes for the moment. He traveled as randomly as he could to evade detection. He didn't dare look behind him, but he feared the screams that could come at any moment.

Chandra darted after them. Gwendolyn appeared in her path, her sword poised. Again, Chandra tried to sidestep the oldest Alcourne, but failed. Finally, she stood upright, hands defiantly on her hips, looking down on the small, pale woman. She raised an eyebrow in something near frustration.

"So be it, if you wish your death now." Chandra crossed her arms. "You know it matters not when I kill *her*—whether in the next moments or the next weeks or the next years. Death comes. Time matters not to me."

"I thought time was too short for you." Gwendolyn regarded Chandra with disgust. "Tell me, Monster. Why do you not allow yourself to take on your true form?

What is there to fear for you then?" Gwendolyn mocked her openly. "Why mask your full power?"

"Clever. This planet doesn't appreciate my true form for long. But perhaps I shall show you a glimpse of reality once again before you die, so that you will know the real fate of your prodigy."

"Perhaps I will not give you the chance!" Gwendolyn cried.

"Large words spoken in hopelessness and fear," Chandra growled. "You have nothing but frail hope in the Unicorn Child, now. I show you real fear. Then I show you an absolute death that you have eluded for so long. Then I kill your last hope as your body quivers in its demise."

Gwendolyn lowered her head in determination, gasping in air through clenched teeth. *Yes, I am afraid of my choice. Yes, I am weak. Yes, I may die. But I will not give up on my hope.* She refused to give up on Ariana. She focused all her internal power on the method that proved her most powerful ability. She began a slow drain on the monster's anger and power. Every strike to Gwendolyn and her opponent would drain more power into Gwendolyn's heart. Every strike would make the creature weaker, she hoped.

"Again with that, Matriarch? Your body is much too old to finish what you have started. This time, you will not be able to handle the power you claim!" Chandra cackled. "So it is death that you choose after all!"

Gwendolyn brought her sword to her side and lunged at the grinning Chandra with all her might. She matched the monster blow for blow, draining the creature with each hit. She felt the power flow into her with uncontrollable speed, giving her a small measure of advantage. She saw Chandra's movements slow as well. She knew that Chandra had not been mistaken in her judgment. Gwendolyn felt on fire with each hit. She decided to at least put up a good fight. She decided to help in this small way. She decided to fight to her death, to her peace.

*   *   *

Ariana stirred on his shoulder, forcing Silvan to slow his pace. He stopped long enough to set her down. The bruise running the length of her face had swollen, but she showed no other ill effects from such a violent encounter with the Monster. He cupped his hand on the uninjured side of her face and put his arms around her, silent sobs tearing from him.

"Gwendolyn?" Ariana gasped.

Silvan nodded. Ariana knew she fought for their freedom. Tears welled in her eyes and dripped down her swollen face, soaking into Silvan's tunic. Her back ached and her face hurt and her joints screamed in pain, but she straightened her shoulders.

"Then we can't waste the time she has bought us. I'm not allowed to die tonight. I have a purpose to fulfill. We have a job to do!" She pulled away from him, trying to be the strong one.

Silvan rubbed at his eyes and smiled at her with his purest emotion, his love for her. "I've made my vow, Ariana. I also think I'm gonna marry you when this is all over!"

"I don't get a proper proposal?" The sweetness in their loving bickering dissolved in the sudden sound that reached them. The passionate and determined gleam in her eyes grew cold and horrified.

Across the miles separating them came a shrill cry of agony and fear so chilling they shivered beneath the warm canopy. It was a warning as much as a death-scream. Gwendolyn, the Matriarch of the Alcourne family, was dying. Her long wail pierced their hearts with such ferocity Ariana almost turned to follow it to her death.

White fire flared in Ariana's waking sight and she saw the entire scene in a vision as it unfolded:

Gwendolyn stood in a glowing aura of white fire. She had dripping gashes all over her body and still she stood. Her pale flesh looked burnt with black patches from which the white fire poured. Chandra staggered and groped impotently for the Matriarch's face. Gwendolyn slashed with her now broken sword at the creature's throat. The slit poured dark blood, but Chandra smiled as blood dripped from her mouth.

"Your limit, Matriarch?" she rasped.

Gwendolyn's eyes widened as more power flowed into her. Her body already brimmed and spewed the power it absorbed. She cried out and groaned with the power, but she pitched forward, lunging at Chandra.

"This power is purified and lost to you, Monster!"

"Always more power to be gained elsewhere!" Chandra replied.

As Gwendolyn stumbled toward Chandra, the Monster reached out with her gauntleted hand and ripped through the Matriarch's stomach. Chandra's hand burst out Gwendolyn's back with a spray of blood and a bright flash of light. Then Gwendolyn screamed with the pain of death and the destruction of the fiery power she had absorbed and took with her into death. Those were the cries they had heard and were still hearing.

Silvan grabbed Ariana, his heart wracked in such anguish that he barely pulled her back. He clamped a hand over her mouth as Ariana began to scream in horror. He shook her to bring her to her senses. The haunted look in Ariana's eyes would not vacate as terrors past and present threatened to cave in on her. Too much loss left her paralyzed. Fear left her paralyzed. Silvan knew she had seen the death of Gwendolyn.

Silvan's violent shaking of Ariana again mobilized her enough to run, and run they did—never stopping, never glancing behind, and always praying that they'd make it just a little longer until they were safe. Into the night their long legs carried them, to a place that was a smudged dot on a vague map in the back of their minds. They hoped they would recognize it when they saw it. They hoped it was for real. They hoped much, for hope was all they had.

Nighttime brought an overwhelming fatigue to the two who had fled death. Their graceful steps faltered and grew heavy. But a tree, a rock formation, and a horizon slowly materialized into something familiar to them. Flatlands eventually became highlands. Foreign became recognizable. The mountain opened into a small, vine-choked cave. The opening was barely a foxhole. Both Ariana and Silvan struggled to squirm through, but the space inside was high enough to stand in and wide enough to lie in. Inside, several containers held stores of food and water. Inside, a narrow tunnel led into pitch-black oblivion. Their spent bodies grew numb. With aching fingers, Silvan pulled the heavy vines back over their hiding place. He pulled thin blankets from dusty boxes. He promised to hide better on the morrow. But fatigue pulled them into a different kind of oblivion. Silvan's last thought held surprise that this sanctuary could really exist. He stared into the darkness.

"Maybe I'm finally dreaming... maybe I'll wake up," Ariana murmured from her curled up position on the ground.

An exhausted Silvan looked at her with sad eyes and brushed back white hair from her bruised face. He pulled the cover up around her neck and stared at her until he almost dozed off. Silvan stared at the mouth of the cave. Blue light suddenly flickered across the opening and drew his eyes upward. Faintly glowing script had appeared and spread across the wall. An intricate seal ranged across the wall, a design he recognized from his lessons. He thought it was just a symbol, but knew he had been mistaken. The seal indicated that a powerful shield had been activated. He could read the old Alcourne text. It translated to:

"Herein and beyond a barrier lies
To protect the innocent from Evil's eyes.
The Sanctuary built of Old
Will now spread an arm
Around the bold kept safe from harm."

A name swirled out beneath the poem. Slowly, the letters unfurled in sweeping strokes. The signature made Silvan gasp. *Love, Gwendolyn, Matriarch of Unicorns.* Along another wall, new lines of pale light cut their way across the stone. Curves and turns and angles soon became a huge map. Silvan stared wide eyed at the rooms and walkways and great halls. The map was larger than any floor plan he'd ever seen, easily three times the size of the mansion in the mountain. The tiny cave fit into the plan, with the hallway leading from it. He stared toward the narrow hallway shrouded in darkness and wondered if a structure of so many levels and of such size could really be housed within the mountain. He would find out the next day.

He lay down between Ariana and the small cave mouth. His hand clasped his sword on the soft sand in front of him. Gwendolyn said this place was safe, protected by unseen forces. But Silvan didn't want to take any chances. He kept a vigilant watch until his body claimed him in sleep. Both Alcournes slept soundly, their dreams and hearts intertwined. Their purpose spread out before them, somehow. The two were all that remained of a great and glorious race with a rich past so amazing it was converted to legend. Their innocence marred by violence, their hearts resolute in righteous anger, they slept unaware that their purpose wove a path for them to the stars.

8: BLESSED BLOOD

Silvan found Ariana where he'd left her, despondent and exhausted after their ordeal. She had curled up in the darkness of the cave for several days, hoping that Chandra would not find them. When they'd both sensed Chandra's weakened presence disappear, she kept them in the cave a day more. Almost a week had passed since her flight from home—Ariana's second real home—and the annihilation of their race. Silvan remained at her side the entire time, determined to keep her afloat. She cried out in her sleep and he held her. She cried while awake and he soothed her. So much loss had brought her to the edge of losing her very sanity. Like a twig, she was bound to break if Silvan didn't do his part to ground her. He'd promised so much and given so much and suffered so much, right alongside her. He knew he would feel this pain one day. But he had to be strong for her, even though his tears fell when she finally slept.

The shock and panic eased. All were dead, save Ariana and Silvan. All were dead so that she could flee. All were dead because a great evil decided to make a gruesome choice. All were dead. Silvan saw the light return to her face one day while he held her close. Her violet-pink eyes lit up with a new passion—not revenge or hatred or self-loathing—for these all had crossed her consciousness. The passion was her honor, her determination, and her purpose. The passion was pure love, the light given her by her dead parents and the hundreds of her kindred who died to ensure that purity could survive. They'd believed. For their belief, they were murdered.

"I will kill that monster, but not for revenge," Ariana said, the first words spoken with clarity in several days. "I will destroy her so that real innocence and love can survive. And I will show her the horror of that power in the face of evil."

Ariana then arose from her apathy. Silvan had spent the previous days delving farther and deeper into the cave they had stayed in. He was determined that the huge map that still glowed on the wall had to be misleading somehow. The entire mountain didn't seem large enough to encase this new fortress. He'd strayed into a fully dark tunnel running both ways. His light always dimmed or his worry over Ariana took over and he would quit for the day. This time, he led her behind him through the narrow corridor, into the blackness.

"Surely it wasn't built in the dark. Is there a light source?" Ariana ran her fingers down the wall.

"Not one that I've found yet."

"Why are you whispering, now?" Ariana sighed. "This is the safest place we could be, right?"

"We've walked forever. The map said there was a door here, but it's just a slick wall." Silvan's dim oil lamp cast dancing light on the blackness.

"Really?" Ariana pursed her lips. "No switch or button or anything?"

She spread her hands across the smooth wall and dragged them down the center, where she figured the partition for double doors would be located. She yelped and jerked her hands away.

"What is it? Are you all right?"

"Something pricked my fingers in the middle." Ariana stuck two fingers into her mouth and sucked to stop the pain. "Just a little, but it hurts!"

She stared at the wall. Silvan swung the lamp to and fro so he could see tiny barbs along the flat surface. Suddenly, a muffled scraping sounded in the corridor, as if beyond the stone on either side of them. A jagged glowing line split the wall where Ariana had touched it. The light was pale, flowing blue, like the map in the front cave. Her jaw dropped open, minor pain forgotten. The wall seemed to groan and complain, but soon began to pull apart along the glowing center. More darkness lay beyond.

"Come on!" Ariana hurried across the threshold.

When she passed through with Silvan in tow, the door began sliding back in place. Silvan gasped and turned just as it closed. A gentle whoosh of air flowed past them, warm and stale. Glowing faintly blue, side rails appeared at each side of their path. Mechanical gears scraped and creaked behind thick stone walls. The hissing of natural gas sounded only seconds before the gas ignited in several torches all along the wall. The light and fire moved in succession down the hall and around the far wall of a huge dome. The rail to their left led into open, empty air. As the light rounded the last few torches in the huge circle, all was still for a moment.

Then, in the perceived void beyond the handrail, pale blue and yellow light erupted from a single source and rained down a lovely glow on several levels of handrails. The chandelier looked organic, like a huge blue willow tree. Each leaf was a pale blue light. Winking in and out along the fronds were yellow lights. Fireflies appeared to be dancing in the willow tree. The beauty held Ariana captivated. She followed the very gentle slope of the walkway. Open doorways of different sizes lit up to her right, some were labeled and some were not.

"Is the writing Gaelic?" Ariana murmured. "I don't understand. It's less refined than the Alcourne script my mother and Aunt Gwen used."

"Must be older science than their generation. Took a blood pact to enter." Silvan glanced back at her. "It knows who you are!"

"It is a bit creepy. Beautiful, but creepy."

A bright blue glow caught Silvan's eye. He faced the doors again. "Hey! Look!"

Ariana turned around. The huge map of the place had reappeared across the closed doors. The writing, thankfully, was in the Alcourne script. She could read it. She saw several sets of rooms designed as living quarters and several for storage. She saw two huge rooms labeled "Food Generation" and pointed.

"You mean you didn't already know of this place beyond the map we memorized?" Ariana was shocked.

"Nope. I've not a clue." He shrugged and leaned toward the map again. "Now that it's close enough to read... Look, this says 'Garden,' too."

"It says there's a garden in the mountain?" Ariana leaned over the rail, peering into the void below. "For actual food?" Her stomach growled, long tired of canned things, sustaining though they were.

"We were told we'd be taken care of." Silvan pointed to the oval labeled 'Garden' in the middle of the map. When he touched the surface, the room he chose had a warm yellow glow around it on the wall. He frowned for a moment.

"I wonder," he said, and ran over to the railing.

"Wait! It's glowing down there! What did you do?" Ariana leaned farther out.

"See? When you touch the map, it lights up and activates the area you chose!"

Silvan pointed to the very bottom of the funneling slope. At the bottom, greenery sprouted before them and came to life from some sort of stasis. The canopy blotted the full garden from view quickly. Ariana dragged Silvan down the sloping walkway of stone to the garden. Their steps wound around the huge dome and finally reached the bottom.

The garden grew abundantly with weeping and graceful trees, rocks, moss and stepping stones. Some flowers bloomed occasionally. The huge garden had naturally hewn stone benches and walkways. A cascading waterfall churned the clear, deep water that filled an irregular pool cut from the existing stone. Seams of uncut precious stones glistened in its surface. Cold water flowed from underground. Ariana cupped her hands for a drink. The water tasted pure and refreshing.

"Hey! Check this out!" Silvan called through the trees.

Ariana followed his voice. More stones had been arranged or cut into shape around a smaller pool of water. The water steamed hot and bubbled up from holes in the bottom of the spring.

"Geothermal heating, too! A hot spring and a cold spring. And the water is forced out along these pathways to water the garden. Not a drop wasted! The engineering is quite simple, but genius." Silvan shook his head. "Our ancestors were really something! The Mansion systems were primitive compared to this!"

Ariana smiled absently at his words, feeling a pang of sorrow in her heart for the Mansion, and turned to the wall above the pool, to where heavy characters had been carved into the stone. She strained to read them. They were etched by heavy but strong hands and read:

"Eternal Sanctuary of the Blessed Blood."

"Eternal, huh? It's sure built to stand the test of time, Ariana. What's wrong?" He put his hands on her shoulders. She trembled all over. "You can tell me."

Ariana stood with her fists clenched at her sides. She bit her lower lip. She dropped her head forward in defeat.

"Why?" she spat. "If this was our ultimate sanctuary, then why didn't they send some of the

Alcourne here in advance of the danger? Fewer would have died. They could have lived!"

"They did, long ago," said a weary voice behind them. "There is only me, now, though."

Ariana screamed when she realized they weren't alone. Silvan had his hands on both swords and ready to draw as he spun around. His jaw dropped and Ariana's eyes widened. The white figure before them stole their breath with her beauty.

"I am glad we are still a fair race, though the form is different, Lady Unicorn." The creature lowered its snout in a curt bow. "So it came to that after all—*everyone* changing like that. And you must be here due to calamity. I see you are the Purposed One."

"I...I...think I dreamed of you once," Ariana stammered.

"We are but a dream to the world, now, my brethren," the weary voice continued. "I felt the loss. I could not see them, but I felt the loss just the same. Now, who remains?"

"We are all," whispered Ariana.

"How is it that you are here, Old One?" Silvan knelt before her. "The others changed long ago."

"Has it been that long? The sleep has lasted this many centuries? I was to wake with your birth, Chosen Unicorn, and I did, but so long since the last!"

Before them stood the creature of lore in original form—much taller than Ariana expected with a coat of purest white, flanks and sides gleaming in the ethereal light, sharp split blue hooves and eyes flooded in deep blue. The white spiral split the flaxen forelock and wound upward from her forehead. Before them, as they both trembled in awe, stood a unicorn from whom they descended. Her mane fell in waves down her neck and shoulders. Her muzzle was mobile and pale pink. She spoke in a ringing voice though her mouth did not move. The sound of her voice simply caressed them so they couldn't tell whether they sensed it in their head or heard it with their ears.

"Oh, my!" Ariana sank to her knees. "Are you real?"

"Oh, yes. Quite real. My light fades but is not extinguished, young one." Her light breath came out in a sigh. "These machines, they preserve only the mind fully. This body has aged. I feel almost transparent with time, though I may look well to your fresh eyes."

"Who are you?" Silvan opened his mouth then closed it again. "I feel," he stammered, "like I should know you."

"My name is Gyllandrea, mother to Sephandrum and Gwendolyn, the children who built this sanctuary." The old one bowed formally. "My Tomb of Life powers this place. Soon, only my spirit will remain to light your way."

"Oh no. Please! Don't go." Ariana pleaded with her eyes. "Too many have gone!"

"You worry too much, young one." Her blue eyes were full of calm. "My spirit will forever be among these walls. Literally."

Silvan stared openmouthed at the unicorn. "G...Gwen! Is that the same person who is Ariana's aunt?"

"Ariana? The child of Celeste? Yes, Gwendolyn is your great-great-great..." Gyllandrea paused. "That explains much as to why you are the Child of Purpose."

"What does it explain?" Silvan's voice was urgent.

"Gwendolyn is the bearer of the great Prophecy, as I was. We take into us a greater portion of life than some of the others in order to see the prophecy reach fruition." Her thin face tilted to the side. "I am sure she told you of the shorter lives of the humanoid unicorns?"

Ariana nodded. "We call ourselves Alcourne, now, but yes." She pulled her body up on the edge of the pool while listening. Silvan sat as well.

Gyllandrea chuckled. "Those unicorns who were born in the form you see before you had naturally longer lives anyway. As unicorns in true form, we maintained our power and near-immortal lives. Then the whole debacle on Atlantis forced us to take drastic measures." Gyllandrea snuffled, her voice irritated. "Since they obviously had to change form to give birth to those already in human form, they kept their power. The gap in power wouldn't have begun until the second and third generation." She drew herself up proudly. "My children were the last born in their natural form, and among the first to undergo the transformation."

Silvan stared wide-eyed. "Gwendolyn really was the first."

Ariana caught his glance and spoke up. "You said 'near-immortal'?"

"Yes, child."

"My dear ancestor! We have horrible news for you. You see, Gwendolyn is dead!"

"No death is absolute, children."

"Forgive my rashness, but we heard her death cries!"

The elder unicorn was quiet for a moment. She lowered her head as if mourning or listening. When she raised her face to them again, her eyes glittered with moisture. Her voice was full of sad laughter.

"Were you taught nothing? Death leaves only a shell. If her shell is broken, then it is by her choice alone! All that is within that shell cannot be destroyed. If possible, she will find her way back to us."

A new wave of sorrow mounted in Ariana's heart. All had died protecting her. Ariana's parents, her aunt, her entire race save these two. The tears brimmed in her eyes again. But how could Gwendolyn not be dead?

"This burden tears into you, but it mustn't break you. For the sake of us all, and the Purposed Ones who came before you! The burden isn't only yours to bear!"

The elder unicorn tilted her head to the side. "Surely Gwendolyn told you this."

"At the end, yes."

Gyllandrea settled her muzzle beside Ariana's face, allowing the young one to place her arms around her neck. Silvan leaned his face against the old one's warm coat. Ariana cried another cleansing round of tears before sobbing to control herself against her grandmother's neck. The older unicorn flooded both of them with such a calming aura of healing that all they felt and heard and thought flowed into blissful contentment. The power was so great that it left them welled with feeling.

"The original power is greater, as you can tell. I will show you how to unlock it within yourself, Purposed One. Perhaps the young man can benefit as well." Gyllandrea jerked her chin toward Silvan with good humor.

Ariana still reeled from the power she'd experienced only minutely from her mother, even as she healed her heart against Death. If her many-times-removed grandmother had so much power in healing, what other abilities lay beneath the surface? As she pulled away from the unicorn, her only family, her hand brushed along a cord around the old one's neck.

"What... is this?"

Gyllandrea stepped closer as Ariana's hand followed the cord to the pendant around her slender neck. A heavy metal cup looped over the black, heavy, worn cord. The pendant that hung there was long and slender—a small piece of alicorn that wound down to a point from the metal cup. Her hand brushed the alicorn. A perfect Spring day in the forest flooded her vision. A shining unicorn stepped into the meadow, followed by a tiny baby, stumbling on spindly legs to catch up. The spirited baby jumped all over the area, always watching behind as his mother walked. A much smaller unicorn baby followed, walking timidly from behind the bushes, with an odd grace that was familiar to Ariana. She saw the baby's eyes.

"I know those eyes!" Tears flowed down Ariana's cheeks again. "Gwendolyn!"

"My babies!" The old one sighed. "You have the gift of flashvision. And this is Gwendolyn's first alicorn, in her true form. It is very powerful. Before you leave on your journey, I wish you to have this piece. I will teach you to use true alicorn."

"I can't possibly take that from you!"

"You will, child." Gyllandrea gave a tilt of her head. "And you'll soon question what is possible."

Ariana bowed her head in courtesy. Then she stared up at Gyllandrea. "Was the boy Sephandrum?" Ariana smiled, remembering his jaunty gait. "I don't recall ever hearing that name before, even in my Alcourne history studies. And Gwendolyn didn't mention him."

"Gwendolyn wouldn't have mentioned him." Gyllandrea shook her head. "They were brilliant from birth, each versed in so many of the old ways. Until the people chose to change shape, to run from their pursuers and live. Sephandrum didn't agree with the decision. He believed we should take our stand, keep our power and our original forms, and fight for equal...or superior...footing among the humans."

"Oh no! So he died for his cause?" Ariana's mind created the vivid image of a frolicking unicorn colt, in love with life, getting struck down brutally.

"Hardly." Gyllandrea laughed heartily, reminding Ariana of Gwendolyn. "Sephandrum helped end the battle for Atlantis. Then he left after building the Sanctuary. He was always a stubborn child. If there is one more alive other than us, it'll be Sephandrum."

Ariana said no more, since she already had so much to mull over. They followed Gyllandrea along the far side of the dome. She took them to a room named the "Crypt of Life" and began their training. Gyllandrea said it was named so because, inside, life went on at over triple the speed of the surrounding world. Training would be more efficient for the short time they have in the outside world when a week equals a month.

"A week of regular time in the world is all we will need." Gyllandrea chuckled to herself. "After that, you can seek your purpose. The fire in you says you also want to put the dead to rest. I ask one thing of you, however, when your purpose is accomplished," she said with all seriousness.

"Anything you ask, dear ancestor," Ariana replied.

"A great-grandchild!" Her voice lilted in laughter.

Silvan stopped and his mouth dropped open. Ariana blushed, surprised at her ancestor's boldness. She realized immediately that Aunt Gwen had her mother's sense of humor.

"Speechless, eh? What's wrong?" Her indignant tone floored Ariana. "Am I going to have to teach you about *that*, too?" Gyllandrea cackled.

This time, Ariana laughed nervously. Silvan finally burst out laughing and put his arm around Ariana's shoulders.

"Well, it's final, Lady Ariana. I've got the blessing of your grandmother. And we can't deprive the world of its most beautiful baby!"

"Silvan!" Ariana's cheeks blazed.

Gyllandrea's laughter flowed back over them like the ringing of bells as the odd door to the time-altering room latched behind them. They faced a barren room with glowing green walls.

Their training began immediately, in basic and advanced methods of purification, in absorption and purification of powerful energies and its dangers. Their trainer was a taskmaster expecting nothing but perfection. She sparred against them with the vigor and strength of youth. Ariana wondered that Gyllandrea showed no signs of her apparent old age, since she'd mentioned before that she felt the drag of time. Ariana wondered how long it would be before *she* began to feel old. *Probably much sooner than this beautiful creature.*

In their studies, the *how* proved much easier than the *do* portion of their training exercises. The old one wouldn't let them rest until they had mastered the task set before them. Gyllandrea taught them how to unlock and use the great speed and strength they had not drawn upon. She took great pains in teaching them advanced plant manipulation, which had been a dying art even when the unicorns were in their original forms. They learned centuries of revelations in weeks. Gyllandrea had so much of the original power and original knowledge that had been lost through the centuries that Ariana set to memorizing everything she was told. By the end of their month-long session, they had gained a lifetime of skills and much wisdom from the ancient one. Gyllandrea told them it was time to re-enter the regular time flow.

"But I haven't learned how to use true alicorn yet!" Ariana said.

Gyllandrea walked over to her and told Ariana to take the cord from her neck and wear it.

"True alicorn, like unicorns in their original form, has more power. Like Mother's first milk, a baby's first alicorn holds a special power. It is like an elixir of life, my grandchild, but cannot be used on the one who produces it," she said.

"You have two—your first alicorn and Gwendolyn's. Both are actually similar in power, from one Purposed One to the next." Gyllandrea's voice brimmed with pride. "You will use them wisely, I know."

"Gwendolyn was a unicorn at full power! She could do so much more! Why didn't she teach me more, then?!"

"Dear child, Gwendolyn is barely younger than I. I was placed in the Tomb of Life and maintained that way. She chose to live in the world, losing more and more of herself each year to keep her body immortal, watching over our people and waiting for you!" Gyllandrea tilted her head to the side in her endearing way. "My son made the same decision. They both possessed little more than a regular humanoid unicorn by the time of your training. As you learned, receiving knowledge and using it are far apart. They may have known more, but would not have been able to show you as I have."

"Do you think we'll ever meet Sephandrum?" Ariana remembered the feasts and celebrations among her kin. She imagined a tall, strong man among them who had Gwendolyn's eyes. But he, like the others, faded in a strong breeze.

"Surely he'll return to the Sanctuary, now that the worst has happened." Silvan shook his head. "But what if he doesn't even know this happened?"

"For all of his bite, if he still lives somewhere in this world, he may return home one day." Gyllandrea sighed again. "And maybe not. Stubbornness is a family trait."

Her eyes grew distant and clouded with memory. Ariana sensed that she shouldn't press for information on him, though a glimmer of hope rose in her chest that still another precious family member may have escaped destruction.

"But about how to use the true alicorn…" Ariana interjected with a soft voice. She dipped her drinking cup in the cold water of the small Crypt of Life spring.

"Ah, yes. Would it be too cliché if I told you that you would know how when the time comes?"

"Yes," she answered honestly.

Her grandmother laughed. "I thought so. Well, each true alicorn has a different 'voice', just like the seedsong only stronger. That 'voice' says different things to different people in different times. Therefore, the 'voice' of the alicorn will tell you how to use it and when to use it, and maybe even what it will do. So when I say you would know how, that is what I mean."

"So I have to learn how to 'listen' to the alicorn? Easy enough."

"Of course, it never speaks until it's time to use it. Quite a quandary."

"All I heard when I first held this alicorn was a baby's laughter and I saw my parents' faces. And with Aunt Gwen's, I saw her walking through the woods and saw her eyes. But it hasn't given me anything beyond that. Neither have."

"All you ever get is an introduction before they are ready to be used. This baby alicorn has been carried for centuries, silent and unused. Waiting for you, too."

"Thank you, Grandmother!" Ariana wrapped her arms around the unicorn's neck, balancing her drink cup and smiling into the unicorn's warm hide.

"Grandmother, huh? You're starting to make me feel old!"

"For a grandmother, you sure kick our butts in battle!" Silvan chimed in, scratching his head. "Are you really okay just staying in this mountain as we leave?"

"Of course I am. I am the only life of this place, the sustainer of power. If I live forever, that is what I promised to do." The note of finality rang in the air. "Oh, and I have to set up a nursery for the baby!"

"The ba...! Let's not get ahead of ourselves, here, Grandmother!" Ariana shrieked, her cup of water almost slipping from her hand.

"Oh, I don't know. I've been thinking of names—Silvan Junior, MacSilvan, Silvanero..." Silvan offered with a grin.

"Okay, young man! If, and I mean IF, we are going to do this, I just decided you're not allowed to hand out any names." Ariana choked on her drink. "And what if it's a girl?"

"Silvania, of course!"

She slapped his shoulder and scolded him soundly. Gyllandrea walked forward and the door to the Crypt of Life unsealed and slid open. Ariana felt the sudden heaviness creep into her limbs. Her heart slowed in its rhythm. The instant they left the room, time seemed to spin to a stop. Even the Old One stepped heavily for a few feet. Ariana's legs felt like they waded through mud. *Is this what the air really feels like? It's like I forgot.*

"Even with the grace, speed and strength you have gained, it will take a few hours to recover from the room's effects." Gyllandrea lifted a hoof very slowly and placed it in front of her with a deliberate motion. "Take care that you measure and control each movement you make. When the 'weight' finally lifts, you may plough headlong into a wall. Gravity inside the Crypt gradually increased throughout your training, but out here you're not as lucky to have a gradual shift."

Silvan ran into the wall three times. Ariana tripped over the root of a plant she swore had been across the room when she took her third step. For all their concentration, their last hours in the Sanctuary of the Blessed Blood were hectic as they frantically gained control over their new speed and strength. Gyllandrea disappeared for a little while, chuckling to herself, but returned with the same amusement glinting in her blue eyes.

"I will be waiting here when you return," Gyllandrea promised. "Your journey is temporary."

That is what Gyllandrea told them. Ariana was sure that 'temporary' meant something different to a creature that seemed eternal. Gyllandrea would reenter the Tomb of Life and place the fortress in stasis in their absence. She nudged Ariana's hand and dropped onto her palm a wooden box carved in the shape of a leaf.

"A gift from Gwendolyn to the next Purposed One," Gyllandrea whispered. "Go ahead, open it."

From the heavy lacquered box, Ariana pulled a long silver chain with a series of strange orange stones along its length. Ariana lifted it into the light. The stones glowed. In the center of each translucent stone rested a single seed.

"She searched for those seeds for much of her life, digging them out of the ground. The prophecy told her where to find the amber that preserved them in perfection," Gyllandrea said. "You will need the special skills I taught you to awaken these ancient seeds. Be sure to listen closely to them."

"I will." Ariana fastened the narrow belt around her hips with her other gear. The dressy amber and silver belt looked oddly out of place with the leather and dark travel clothes, but Ariana wore it proudly, wondering at the care taken in creating it.

They shared a tearful goodbye. Both Silvan and Ariana clung to their great grandmother as tears streamed down their faces in gratitude and sorrow. Then they left through the great stone doors and out the tiny cave mouth.

Burying the dead was the first step of their journey. Then they would seek out their Purpose together. Months or years could pass before they returned. Ariana was certain that time would change so much more about her life, so she fought the urge to stay in the Sanctuary. She was also curious. In the midst of her righteous determination to fulfill her purpose, she still wanted to know if her uncle lived. Would he answer to that name, *Sephandrum*? Would she recognize Sephandrum if she found him? If life on other planets existed, could he have journeyed beyond the stars? Her plight suggested that hers would be that kind of journey since Chandra's aura had completely gone from this planet. They couldn't be foolish enough to think she was dead.

They retraced steps to the barren place where Gwendolyn had given her life to allow them one last chance at survival. They found no trace of that body, which unsettled Ariana. The entire area was charred. Had Gwendolyn's body been burnt to ashes? They couldn't tell from the remnants. Nothing substantial remained. Ariana was careful not to place too much hope in the absence of a body. But the glimmer flared now and then. Hope was her ally. From Chandra's black memorial, they continued the long journey through the lands of their ancestors.

They ventured to their homelands and came upon more nightmarish places running red with the blood of her kinsmen. The sturdy bodies had only just begun to decay, but no animals dared disgrace an Alcourne's body by using it for food.

They spent whole days burying the Alcournes who had resisted, some whom Ariana only barely remembered or couldn't recognize. The stench of decay hung in the air more strongly as the days went on. They moved corpses and buried them and moved corpses and buried them. She wondered if they should instead burn the bodies. Silvan gave a stern no to that question. Alcournes are always to be buried. To burn them sends their power into the sky, destroying it, instead of within the earth where it belongs.

Desecration of the bodies in each location seemed worse than that encountered only the day before. Decay was stronger, too. Ariana had to bury her self-pity in the first grave she dug. She bit her lip in some internal struggle every now and again, but did not speak much during these hard days.

The last place they sought out was the Mansion in the Mountain. All those who surrounded Silvan since infancy had been butchered. Those he loved as family lay where they fell, their blood soaked into the ground and rock. The worst decay displayed in open air was a final insult to creatures that were once almost eternal. Silvan finally broke down in the place of his youth. Silvan fell down on his face in front of the door of the

Mansion, with Ariana's arms clutching him tightly. They shook and quivered when they regained control of their tears. Their bleary red eyes stared all around them as the great swells of paralyzing sorrow died away.

Ariana and Silvan searched the Mansion for victims. Stale smoke burned Ariana's nose when she wandered into the charred library. So much lost, and Chandra took the books from them as well. Nothing of great importance had been left intact, it seemed. Then something caught her eye behind a toppled bookcase. Silvan pushed the furniture aside with ease.

"I'm still not accustomed to this strength." Silvan stared at his hands.

"Me, neither." Then Ariana leaned toward the wall. She traced the edges of a rectangular indention. "Odd that it's there. Can you open it?"

Ariana stood back. Silvan dislodged the thin stone front, letting it crash on the floor. Behind the stone was a metal safe. Silvan grasped the handle and snapped the door off in one motion. He stared at Ariana.

She smiled at him. "It is impressive, this new strength." He blushed, the awkwardness creeping into his posture. Ariana reached past him into the vault. Triumphant and beaming, she pulled out a thick book. It stank of smoke, but she sighed in relief. The history of the Alcourne family was intact in her hands.

"I guess that's one thing they'd like to have." Silvan touched the cover with reverence.

Ariana nodded. "This book belongs in the Sanctuary. We'll see that it makes it there after this is over. And after we've learned what we can from it."

Tucking the book into her pack, Ariana followed drops of dried blood to her room, only to find her mother's marble jewelry box shattered on the stone floor. The head and footboards of the bed had been snapped and the mirror had long cracks in the glass from the force of a careless punch. Ariana was numb to the loss of things. *Things* could be replaced, but for the one item she sought in her bedroom.

She had taken great pains to hide it well, and the monster had almost found it. Ariana climbed over the broken furniture to the little vanity table she never used. She dug her fingernails under the thin inlaid top and felt surprised when the wood splintered under her fingers. Her new strength made her hiding place seem insignificant as she ripped off the vanity's top to reveal a thin wooden matchbox in between the layers of lumber. She grabbed the matchbox frantically and slid off the cover. Dark blue cloth shone in the sunlight. Ariana grabbed the tiny pouch with angel wings and clutched it to her breast. Love's pouch, the Angel's burden carried until the day she died. She turned and left the broken room.

They buried all the dead at the mansion in the sacred cemetery with Ariana's parents. Ariana looked around sadly at the destruction. The trees, forever blooming, wilted. The flowers drooped to the soil, dying in the cold winter air. The façade of the great dwelling with its now-leafless wisteria twining up the sides had been painted with the red blood of her newly claimed ancestry. The plant life mourned the loss of the sustaining power unto death. Both the remaining Alcournes thought that a fitting tribute from nature.

Ariana knelt on the ground with her mother's broken finger bones laying on her lap. Numb to the desecration after so much suffering, she couldn't shed another tear. Ariana settled by her mother's grave, having one last bout of tired bitterness at the sacrilege of stealing the blood ruby from the Angel's hand. One last longing to know what that jewel would teach her. She said a small prayer and mended the grave of her mother, rejoining her hand with her body. Ariana gathered the seeds from her parents' graves into the blue pouch with angel wings and tied the pouch around her neck. Then she stood among the hundred graves they had dug to fill the clearing.

She sank her bare feet into the dirt and reached for Silvan's hand. She spread her hands to her sides, nodded to him and closed her eyes. Their energy poured into the ground to flood the burial place with the life of the trees and flowers. The seedsong rang through the air, billowing and receding like a gentle breeze. They opened their eyes on the most ornate and expansive floral ceremony ever in this place of peace and rest, using everyone's seed pouches. They should have been drained and exhausted by their constant burials, but each only felt a comfortable drain on their new reserves of stamina. For nearly an hour, they gazed on the lovely flowers, on the petals streaming in the spring-like breeze.

Ariana startled when she heard a crackle of far-away limbs. Silvan was on his feet, weary but looking for a plan of flight.

"We will wait," Ariana said simply.

Silvan relaxed and nodded while pulling at her wrist. "But not in the open."

Ariana allowed herself to be led into the cover of the forest, away from her sorrow. *Yes,* she thought, *we will wait. We have waited this long. And now, our path comes to meet us.*

Ready for more? The story continues in
Primorda, Book 5, A Novella of the Pathos Series,
Available in Kindle Unlimited, Audible, and Paperback
In Fall of 2026!

ABOUT THE AUTHOR

Tamara Henson lives in Kentucky with her precious little family, and all the people in her head. She's devoted to her son Elric and her man Will, and her kitty-brat Twitter-pater. She's a Sci-fi/Fantasy Author and Artist, Anime/Manga Fan, Legal Stabber of Tattoo and Piercing Clients, a Directionally-Challenged and Incompetent Gamer Gal, and a Workaholic Entrepreneur. Always improving, except in gaming, probably.

She is likely working on something creative, when she should be sleeping.

To access exclusive info and offers related to Tamara's PATHOS universe, go to her website:

www.tamarahenson.com

Discover other Pathos Series titles by Tamara Henson:

- Rowan Jun (Book 1)
- Silver Empress (Pathos, Book 2)
- Solana (Pathos, Book 3, A Novella)
- Primorda (Book 5) *Fall, 2026*
- Incarnata (Book 6) *Spring, 2027*

Discover 3 NEW Romance Series by Tamara Henson (Series Titles TBA):

Cryptid (w/ a JACKALOPE SHIFTER!!), *Fall, 2026*
Dystopian and Dark Fae Romance Series
TITLES TO BE ANNOUNCED, COMING SOON!

<u>ABOUT THE PATHOS SERIES:</u>

Tamara Henson's ever-expanding Pathos universe spans space and dimensions beyond the waking world to bring fresh life to mythologies, folklore, and legends, spinning epic original locations and memorable, multi-dimensional characters in rich detail with her playful dialogue and direct writing style.

Join Rowan Jun in his path toward redemption from slave to warrior.

Walk the path of Briescha, a born diplomat so dedicated to her sister that she would shatter the cosmos to keep her safe.

Follow Solana into the wilderness as she escapes those who seek to harm her, and follows the voice of the mysterious Taiyo of the Flames.

Let Ariana guide you through her new life in the Mansion in the Mountain, where the mystery of her family is finally revealed, and her true trial begins.

Tread the path toward life and redemption, where suffering and pain hold the promise of a brighter, more joyful future. The Pathos Series!

Join the tamarahenson.com newsletter for updates on all Tamara's Upcoming Projects!

ARIANA